Perfect SURRENDER

MIA LONDON

Perfect Surrender

by Mia London

This is a work of fiction. Names, characters, places and incidents either are the product of the author's imagination or are used factitiously, and any resemblance to actual persons, living or dead, business establishments, event or locales is entirely coincidental.

ISBN 978-0-9905274-5-9

Publisher: Mia London
PO Box 93852
Southlake, TX 76092

Cover photo by Shutterstock.

Cover design by JLH Designs.

ACKNOWLEDGEMENTS:

ii

Sandy, Lisa and Ren. I couldn't have done it without you.

<h1 style="text-align:center">CHAPTER ONE</h1>

THE EIGHT-HOUR flight to Paris gave Lauren plenty of time to think about what she was leaving behind for the next four weeks.

She trusted her brother. She did. More than anyone else on the planet. But that didn't mean she wouldn't worry about the spa and how he'd run it in her absence.

Lauren Knight landed in Paris, ambled with the crowd to baggage claim, and saw a man who held up a sign with her name on it. Mr. Bernard, she presumed. He was her aunt's attorney, and from the phone conversations, he had a congenial disposition. Close to her aunt's age, he was an older gentleman with gray hair and bright eyes.

"*Mademoiselle* Knight. I'm Louis Bernard. Welcome to Paris. I hope you found your flight pleasant." How she adored the French accent.

"Hello, Mr. Bernard. Thank you, and please call me Lauren." The corner of her lips curved.

He nodded, his smile beamed. "*Oui*. If you please, our car is out front," he said as he reached down and lifted her suitcase.

Lauren felt bad that he carried her suitcase.

She knew it would be heavy. She overpacked trying to be prepared for anything, weather, meetings, maybe touring.

The driver greeted them at the curb, immediately retrieved her luggage from Mr. Bernard and hoisted it into the trunk of the car. Then the driver opened the back door for her. She sidled in next to the already seated Mr. Bernard.

"I am sure you are tired from the flight. The jet lag can be quite unbearable. I will have the driver take you to your hotel, not far from our offices, and pick you up in the morning as well. Shall we say ten o'clock?"

"As much as I am anxious to get started Mr. Bernard, I believe you are correct. I should rest and start fresh in the morning. I would also like to see my aunt's house, if you can take me sometime soon."

He nodded several times. "*Oui. Oui.* We will do that the day after tomorrow. Tomorrow, however, we shall go over her will and the financial handlers will discuss her holdings with you as well."

The drive to the hotel was amazing. Or maybe it just seemed that way because Lauren dreamed about coming to Paris someday and now she was here. She lived in New York her whole life and, aside from Niagara Falls, she'd never been out of the country, until now. Excitement tingled throughout her whole body.

She had studied French for three years in high school because she loved the sound of it to her ears. She often dreamed of coming to France, specifically Paris. Now she was here.

The car passed old and new buildings alike,

statues, and many people walking the sidewalks. After about thirty minutes, the Eiffel Tower came into view. Momentous, graceful and majestic. The curves of her lips rose, and she sighed. This is really happening, she thought. *I'm here.*

***

The driver waited for Lauren at precisely ten o'clock the next morning to take her to the law offices of Mr. Bernard.

"Good morning, Lauren," Mr. Bernard greeted her at the lobby of his office. "Would you please follow me?"

They walked to a conference with a large table, several chairs, and a view of downtown Paris.

"Can I get you something to drink? Coffee? Water?"

"No, thank you. I'm fine," she smiled.

After getting comfortable in his office, Mr. Bernard opened a folder in front of him and proceeded to read her aunt's will.

Although Lauren wasn't close to her aunt, she knew her aunt and her mother were close. Despite herself, she felt a stream of melancholy come over her. One of her family members, her mom's only sister, had died. What a sad, isolating thought.

A shiver swept through Lauren.

She tried to focus her attention back to Mr. Bernard. He answered her few questions. With the exception of a handful of charitable organizations, there were no other heirs except herself and Cole. Thankfully, everything was rather straightforward.

To Lauren's great surprise, Mr. Bernard also

asked about a memorial service for her aunt.

"Oh dear. I haven't even thought about that. I recall you said she wished to be cremated, and . . . I guess I just forgot."

"Not to worry, *Mademoiselle* Lauren, I will arrange for a service at a hall in Paris, say next week?" His eyebrows rose as he asked her the question.

"Yes, that would be excellent. However, I don't know how to contact any of my aunt's friends."

"Leave that to me," he said smiling. And she would. She was coming to trust Mr. Bernard with most everything related to the inheritance and her aunt's death, but did she have another choice?

After lunch, the financial advisors arrived and proceeded to enumerate her aunt's holdings. The gentlemen were patient with her as she struggled to understand what they told her.

Overwhelmed didn't begin to describe what Lauren felt after her first day of meetings. She stood and rubbed her aching temples.

As she gathered her documents, Mr. Bernard came into the conference room where she had met with everyone. He assured her they would take a trip to her aunt's house in the outskirts of Paris the next day.

"*Mademoiselle* Lauren, there is just one last thing."

She turned to see him approach holding an envelope in his hand.

"This is a letter your aunt has written for you. Please take it with you, and perhaps you can read it at your hotel."

She glanced down at the letter and took it from him. "Thank you, Mr. Bernard. I will."

Once back at the hotel Lauren sent off an email to her brother, Cole, brushed her teeth and got ready for bed.

She plopped herself on the bed and settled in to read her aunt's letter.

My dearest Lauren,

If you are reading this, that certainly means something unexpected has happened to me. Well, no worries, dear. I am only too happy to leave some money for you and your brother so that you can throw a party and celebrate. My dear attorney, Thomas Bernard, whom you've undoubtedly met, will fill you in on all the details.

The reason for this letter, I must tell you, is primarily a confession of sorts. I feel only regret and sorrow about your mother and father's death.

I loved your mother and instantly took a liking to your father when she brought him home so many years ago. When your mother told us she was getting married, we couldn't have been happier. She was a wonderful woman and deserved all the happiness in the world.

What I never told anyone was that her death ripped my heart out. She was taken from us far too soon. And to make it worse, I know I took her for granted.

I moved to Paris shortly after your

parents married. It was supposed to be a temporary thing, but I ended up staying. I kept in touch with Sylvie, but it was not enough.

She came to Paris once to visit, but couldn't do it again after you and Colton were born. I knew the responsibility then lay with me to visit more often, but my trips became fewer and fewer. And when I decided to make a Christmas trip, it was too late.

Of course, my thoughts focused on you and your brother. Who would care for you?

I talked to your uncle on your father's side, and he made it clear had no concerns about taking you two in and raising you in New York.

I must confess I felt relieved. Not because I didn't want to raise you. You two were darlings—fun, full of life, curious and a joy to be around. No, I was concerned that seeing you both every day would remind me of everything I lost when I lost your mother, my sister. Especially with you, Lauren. You look so much like your beautiful mother it is positively frightening. I knew I wasn't strong enough to raise you properly and face my pain. All I can hope is that you forgive me.

When I returned to Paris, I was determined to throw myself into life. And I mean literally—you shall find photo books of my skydiving and other adventures at the house. I did it mostly to forget the early death of my sister, but partly to test the gods. I wasn't sure I deserved to live.

With the help of my financial advisors, I made a lot of money, bought a big house, hosted many parties for my friends, and traveled the world multiple times over. I fell in love a dozen times, made love to two dozen men, and never regretted a moment of it.

My only regret was regarding Sylvie. And that's all I can ask of you and Colton. Have no regrets. Live life to the fullest. Fulfill your wildest dreams, and I'm hoping a little money will help you do just that.

You two are so precious to me. I want only the best for both of you.

All my love,
Aunt Rosie

Lauren peered into the envelope and found a picture of her mother and aunt, smiling as they posed in front of a Ferris wheel. They were about twenty.

Tears streamed down Lauren's cheeks unbidden. Her aunt was right. She looked exactly like her mother.

Reading the letter brought a flood of memories back for Lauren. She was eleven when her parents died in a car accident, Cole only six. For his sake, she kept her mourning mostly to herself. And through the years, she'd learned to push down the sorrow and pain because it was simply too much to handle. But regrettably it never went away.

She yanked the curtains closed because, despite the fact that it was ten at night, the sun was still out. She returned to the bed, switched off the light, and covered her head to drown the sobs that spilled from her mouth.

She missed her parents terribly and now mourned for an aunt she hardly knew.

She cried herself to sleep.

CHAPTER TWO

LAUREN AWOKE feeling exhausted after a restless night. The bags under her eyes were evident when she looked in the mirror.

"Pull it together," she told the reflection.

After breakfast and an extra cup of coffee, Lauren started to feel a little more human and actually looked forward to visiting her aunt's house.

She strolled outside the hotel and met Mr. Bernard.

"*Bonjour, mademoiselle.*"

"Good morning, Mr. Bernard."

"Are you ready to see the house today?"

"Yes," she smiled at him.

The driver took them outside the city, away from the many buildings, into a residential area. The homes were mostly older stone homes. Exactly the kind of style Lauren had seen in pictures and had visualized. It made her smile.

The car pulled up to the curb in front of a large, stone house and parked the car. A low stone fence with a little iron gate surrounded the property.

Mr. Bernard held open the little iron gate, and

Lauren passed through. Her eyes traveled the exterior of the house as Mr. Bernard unlocked the front door.

The white stone was cut and stacked to form over-sized bricks. She noticed a few spots with mildew that could be removed easily with a good scrubbing. The dark roof had two little dormers peering down at her. The landscaping across the front was lush but overgrown in spots. The tall wooden door had glass and iron insets that made a welcoming and impressive statement. The most interesting part of the exterior, though, had to be the blue wooden shutters. The color was captivating and played well with the vintage house.

She walked past the two potted plants, up three steps, and into the foyer. Lauren gasped. *Wow!*

Her aunt appeared to have eclectic taste. The word *bold* came to mind. Large tiles of black and white laid on the floor from the front door and into the rest of the house. Her eyes followed the curved staircase to the second floor and an enormous chandelier overhead.

She caught a look into the dining room to the right. Another large room. And her jaw went slack at the vibrant blue walls in the living room.

Mr. Bernard jarred her thoughts.

"Lauren, take your time to look around. You may have noticed from the two dormers there is an attic. And the car garage is in the back."

The door opened, and the driver brought in a stack of boxes and paper.

"Straight down that hall, Jon, and place them in the kitchen." Turning to her, he said, "The real estate agent will come to the house at two o'clock. Her name is Corinne Marceille. She is very good. She will also give you tips on preparing the house. I will be at my office if you need me. Otherwise, I shall pick you up later."

She nodded. "Thank you. I'll see you at five o'clock."

"*Absolument*," he smiled and walked out, closing the door behind him.

Lauren took a deep breath. She looked to her right and saw a formal dining room with a large cherry table and twelve chairs. *Goodness.*

Across the foyer was the formal living room. Colorful walls, but certainly a spacious room. She continued to the kitchen where her aunt kept the black and white theme—black and white tile floor, white cabinetry, and black granite countertops. Was black and white popular in France?

Lauren meandered through the whole house. She counted six bedrooms, seven bathrooms, a sunroom, and a butler's pantry. As large as the house was, Lauren couldn't deny the unquestionably cozy feel in the place. The atmosphere seemed joyful. She could imagine living in a home like this one day, although she'd have to leave Manhattan for that.

Her goal today focused on boxing some things that could go to a church or someplace for donation.

Now, where to start?

Probably best to start downstairs and work her way up. Lauren knew it would be overwhelming, but taking it a room at a time, she would be able to handle it.

Her mother used to tell her, "Lauren, how do you eat an elephant? One bite at a time." This house project was certainly an elephant. Not to mention, this was just the first day of several. She didn't need to stress herself out about getting everything done today.

The kitchen would probably be the easiest place to start. Lauren pushed up her sleeves and opened the cupboards. She took down plates, bowls, saucers, and wrapped them in the paper. She peeked into anything with a lid. Didn't people hide valuables sometimes in pots, pans, and cans? It didn't appear that anything of value lay hidden behind those doors. She did scope out some soup that she could make for lunch. At least she thought it was soup since the label read *soupe.*

At two o'clock, the doorbell rang. *What a jaunty little chime.*

She opened the door for the real estate agent.

"Hello, *Mademoiselle* Knight. I am Corinne Marceille," she smiled as she extended her hand.

"Hello, Corinne. Please call me Lauren," she shook the woman's hand.

"So great to meet you. I am sorry about your loss."

She noticed Corinne's English was quite good. "Thank you. Come in, won't you?"

"What a very spacious house."

Is that code for this house needs an overhaul before it can sell?

"Yes. It appears my aunt had very eclectic tastes."

"Indeed. Why don't you show me around?"

After the thorough tour, the ladies sat at the kitchen table, and Corinne opened her notebook.

"So tell me, how long will you be in Paris, Lauren?"

"I'll be here for four weeks."

"Excellent. Here are my initial thoughts. The

house is spacious, and that sells." She leaned in a little like she was telling Lauren a big secret. "We like our big houses, just like you Americans do," she grinned.

"We are finding larger homes are becoming more and more appealing because they can accommodate multiple generations."

"Ah." Lauren understood that. Elderly parents would come live with their adult children, especially if they needed help.

"Now for the downside."

Lauren's face fell.

"Oh, no," Corinne reassured her. "It's not horrific. Some of the color we might need to tone down, that's all."

"Oh, yes. I had expected that."

"I advise you not to clear everything away. Furniture will help to stage the house," she informed Lauren. "This is a very appealing house in an appealing location. It is old but has character, and the electrical, plumbing and windows appear to have been updated, so this should sell fast." Corinne slid her contract towards Lauren.

"That was just the kind of news I was looking to hear."

She reviewed the contract, thankful it was in English and signed it.

She and Corinne shook hands and set a date when Corinne could come back and take pictures. After Corinne left, Lauren returned to her chores and to finish up her day.

Three-thirty, already?

She made a list of things to remember and requests for Mr. Bernard, the highest priority being painters. A few rooms needed a neutral paint color on the walls, others just needed touching up.

She rolled her shoulders and stood to box more kitchen items.

Cole called her before dinner and, even as tired as she was, she did her best to sound optimistic.

"Hello?"

"Hey sis, how's it going in Paris?" He sounded upbeat, and that was what Lauren hoped to hear. Acting gay to take over as manager of the spa was surely no small feat.

"Hey, Cole. It's great here. I love this city."

"I'm glad to hear it."

"Basically, I don't have much to report. I've met with the lawyer and the financial people. There will be more meetings, no doubt, but transferring assets to the US shouldn't be a huge deal. I took a tour of her house, or should I say, mansion."

"No way."

"Way. Aunt Rosie had apparently invested wisely and was able to buy a huge house. So now I need to go through her things and sort everything in order to get the house ready to sell. Plus, I will need to host a memorial service for her."

"How are you supposed to do that?"

"Well, the lawyer is going to help me. Apparently they were friends. Maybe even more than friends, if you know what I mean." Lauren smiled recalling her aunt's letter about her *boyfriends*.

"Yes, I know what you mean."

"Anyway, that's pretty much all I have. I'm trying to adjust to the longer days here. It's strange seeing the sun set at ten o'clock." She chuckled.

"Well, it's almost dinnertime for you, right?

Why don't you go order a hamburger? I heard they put a fried egg on it."

She laughed again. "It's true. So how is everything at the spa?"

"Very good. Nothing to report. 'Course, it's only been one whole day without you."

"Oh, that's right. Well, I'll let you go. Mrs. Prestavich will likely be in this week. Remember she's going through a divorce, so treat her with kid gloves."

"I haven't forgotten. You take care of everything in Paris and get home soon."

"I will. Love you."

"Love you back." She hung up the phone, and mentally patted herself on the back.

She thought she sounded reasonably cheery. More than anything, she wanted to show Cole she was confident he could run the spa. He had stepped outside his comfort zone on so many levels when he agreed to this. She needed him to know she believed in him. Plain and simple.

CHAPTER THREE

WHO KNEW CLOSING out an estate and selling a home of a deceased relative could be so hard? She must have looked haggard, when Mr. Bernard felt compelled to tell Lauren to take a break, relax, and go sightseeing for the day.

The good news was Lauren knew right where to go first.

She jumped off the bus in front of the Eiffel Tower and gasped at its sheer size. She slowly walked the base of the structure and looked up. Everything about the tower was gigantic—the beams, the rivets, the designs in the steel. What an awesome sight. And the day was absolutely clear, so she had no doubt visibility would be miles. After several minutes, she stepped to the ticket counter.

"*Bonjour*," the agent said.

"*Bonjour*," she replied. "One, please."

The agent printed the ticket and, seeing that she was American, pointed to the mini-screen displaying the amount in Euros. Then the agent said something Lauren couldn't make out.

"Excuse me?"

The agent repeated something about the second floor before going to the top. What did she mean? Lauren bit her lip. She glanced back and saw the line had increased. She could not ask the agent again to repeat herself. Instead, she just smiled and said, "Okay. *Merci.*"

She got in the shorter line that formed in front of the elevator. That would be a good place to start. If she were in the wrong area, perhaps someone else could direct her where she needed to go.

She entered the huge elevator with about twenty other people, clutching her bag in close, and backed against a wall.

A tall Frenchman entered after her and briefly made eye contact. He stood over six-foot tall, with dark brown hair and lean, muscular shoulders and arms. He carried a satchel that looked like a camera case. Perhaps she'd been wrong—maybe the tall, handsome stranger was a tourist and not French at all. He smiled at her. She nodded and looked away.

She flushed, but all was forgotten the moment the elevator lurched upward and her stomach did a flip-flop. Lauren found herself holding her breath.

The elevator stopped on the second floor. Okay, she thought. This is what the attendant meant downstairs. She exited and took in the view. It certainly seemed higher than two stories. She could see the area where her hotel was located. She could also spy several other sites she wanted to visit while in Paris.

Behind her, she heard a group of people pass and proceed to a line for another elevator. She presumed that would take her to the top. A thousand feet up. She clutched her purse harder. She took in a reinforcing breath and stepped onto the elevator.

It climbed and climbed. Finally, it stopped. Lauren walked onto the platform faster than she would have liked as the group of anxious tourists carried her. Immediately, she gasped.

Oh my God.

She hugged the wall and peered out. The view was spectacular. The skies were clear, and she could see forever. However, her feet wouldn't move, and her heart hammered in her chest like a racehorse. She blotted the perspiration at her lip. She cautiously walked a few feet, frequently pausing, when the tall French-looking tourist caught her eye. He appeared to be taking pictures.

She made her way, slowly walking the platform, but away from the outer railing. She stopped against the wall, still breathing heavier than usual. Lauren closed her eyes for a brief moment and took a calming breath. She had no idea her fear of heights was this extreme. She read somewhere that fear of height was worse among controlling people. She wasn't a control freak, was she?

Perhaps it would be best if she turned around and rode the elevator back to the second floor.

"Hello," she heard from her right side.

She opened her eyes and turned to see the French-looking tourist standing beside her. He was indeed tall, six-two she guessed, with medium olive skin and dark brown hair. He had a notable French accent.

"Hello."

"Are you afraid of heights?" he asked with a small smile on his face.

She grimaced. "Yes, I do believe I am."

"I see." After a brief pause, he offered her his hand. "I'm Andre Beauchamp."

Despite herself, Lauren couldn't help finding Andre, and his accent, vastly appealing. When he smiled, the slightest dimple showed on his face and his eyes were the most welcoming shade of chocolate. She was impressed by his upper body physique—muscular chest, shoulders and arms, but not bulky. She resisted letting her eyes roam his entire body.

"Lauren Knight," she smiled back at him.

He glanced out at the expanse of Paris, and back at her. "Well, perhaps I can appeal to your sense of logic."

She raised an eyebrow.

"Like many tall buildings, the *Tour d'Eiffel* is specifically engineered to be as sturdy and secure as possible."

She hesitantly smiled. "That's true."

"I imagine it took you some courage to make it all the way up here, yes?"

She nodded. "Yes."

"And it would be very sad if you had to go down without a good look around, no?"

She nodded again.

"How about I walk with you closer to the metal railing and tell you what you are looking at?"

She licked her lips. Could she do this? She wasn't going to fall. She wasn't going to be blown off by the wind. The building wasn't going to crumble to the ground. Dear Lord, she had to do this or look like an imbecile in front of this very handsome Frenchman.

"Okay," she replied.

He held out his hand to her. She hadn't expected that. Her hands were sweaty. She wiped her right palm across her pants and slipped her hand into his. Almost instantly, some relief from the anxiety swept through her body.

Andre proceeded closer to the railing. He seemed to know she needed to walk slowly.

"Look out. See there." He stretched his arm and pointed. "That is the *Champ de Mars*." She noticed how he placed himself between her and the railing.

They walked some more. He held her hand the whole time. He pointed out the *Arc de Triomphe*, *Notre Dame*, the *Louvre*, and, of course, *La Seine* River. Buildings, bridges, cars appeared so small— Lauren refused to think about how high up she was. Once he gently told her not to look directly down.

He snapped a few pictures of her with Paris in the background. She forced a relaxed smile.

"Have you seen enough?"

Oh, God, yes. "I think so."

"How about some lunch? Do you have lunch plans?"

She didn't glance at her watch, but Lauren was fairly certain it wasn't even eleven.

"Okay. No. No plans."

And really, what was it with the monosyllabic word answers? The sooner she got off this monstrosity of steel in the sky the better, because evidently her vocabulary remained on the ground, in addition to her common sense.

When they walked off the elevator, she immediately exhaled and felt her shoulders relax. He continued to hold her hand, and because she didn't want to embarrass herself any further, she asked, "May I have my hand back?"

He looked down as if he'd forgotten he held it almost the whole time. He smiled and released it.

"I'm sorry."

She meekly smiled and wiped her palms against her twill pants. "It's okay." As her senses returned, she recalled that they planned to go to lunch. "So where shall we go eat?"

He smiled showing his lovely dimple again. "I've got a place in mind a few blocks from here. It has a little bit of everything."

"That sounds good to me." And as they walked she snagged a glimpse of the time. Twelve-thirty! *Goodness! How can it be this late?*

"So you're American, yes, Lauren?"

"Yes, and you are French?"

"*Oui*. I was born in the South of France and moved here to Paris to attend the University and, after graduation, decided to stay. So what do you?"

"I manage a spa in New York."

"That must be fun. Do you get many celebrities?"

She smiled. It was funny how people thought of that. "Yes, we do. Mostly those that live in the city, but occasionally we get celebrities passing through town for work or leisure. What do you do, Andre?"

"I'm a photographer."

"Now, that sounds like a fun job."

The conversation ceased momentarily as they arrived at a little café with an open-air feel because the wall was pushed and folded back to each side. Andre spoke to the hostess, who waved her hand over the restaurant as she spoke back.

He motioned Lauren to take a table outside, tucked in a corner. "We can sit anywhere we like. How is this?" he asked.

"This looks lovely."

As lovely as you, he thought.

When Andre decided to take the day and wander around, do some people-watching, he had no idea he'd see such a lovely American woman in his city. She had wavy, shoulder-length light brown hair and was one meter, seventy centimeters tall, he estimated. Her movements had such grace to them. He surprised himself as he tracked her from the ticket counter at the *Tour d'Eiffel* to the elevator. His fascination with her baffled him.

Merde!

Considering he intended to go to the top, he purchased a ticket. *What the hell.* But from that point, he couldn't stop himself from seeking her out.

Damn it, he scolded himself. He had no business seeing out an American woman who was unquestionably here on vacation.

When he caught sight of her pressed against the wall, he knew she was afraid. She looked so precious trying to compose herself.

He was determined to meet her. And here he sat with her beautiful face smiling back at him. He could have kicked himself for inviting her to lunch.

"So what kind of photographer are you?" she asked smiling brightly. The way her eyes twinkled and her lips gracefully curved, he very quickly grew to like her smile. It made her eyes crinkle so gently. He could imagine placing kisses on those crinkles. Her whole face actually. *Mon Dieu.*

"I'm a photographer for travel magazines and books."

"That sounds exciting. Have you photographed the Eiffel Tower before?" She looked so adorable the way her nose scrunched up in bewilderment.

"I have. Multiple times. This trip up was mostly for pleasure. I have a few days before I leave again on assignment, and with the sky so clear, the opportunity was too good to pass up." He glanced at her smiling face and added, "I'm glad I did."

The blush across her cheeks was subtle and gave her such an innocent look, he wanted to capture it. But somehow he knew pulling out his camera in that little café would make her uncomfortable.

"So where are some places you've been? What pictures have you taken?"

"I've been to quite a lot of places. Several you might expect like the Great Wall of China, the pyramids of Egypt, the Sydney Opera House, the Capilano Suspension Bridge in Vancouver. And some exotic places like Victoria Falls, Zambia, and Borobudur, Indonesia."

Her eyes went wide. "You have certainly been around the world. Have you ever photographed places in the United States?"

"*Oui.* I've shot churches in New England, The Alamo in San Antonio, the Golden Gate Bridge. I have the most amazing shot of Antelope Canyon in Arizona."

The curve of her lips gently pushed upward. "You live a very exciting life, Andre," she said.

He shrugged a shoulder. "I suppose I do. We don't often think about it when we're in the midst of it, no? Something about taking life for granted?"

She nodded. "Yes, it's true. So where are you off to next?"

The waiter set down a liter of water and asked for their orders. Andre ordered a tapenade spread with a baguette.

"I ordered an olive tapenade to start. It's delicious. I hope that is okay."

"Yes. Thank you."

"To answer your question, I'm going to Greenland. The government wants me to be part of an expedition to document glaciers."

She tipped her head, and her shiny light brown hair fell over her shoulder.

"I was there this time last year, so I will return to the same location," he continued. "There is great concern about the ice loss. I will work with climatologists and other scientists who will be recording the changes."

"So you are documenting global warming?"

"Yes."

She nodded. "That's seems interesting."

"Then, I get a little break before heading to Croatia to photograph the Brela Beach. After that, I fly to Spain. I will be there during the running of the bulls."

"How exciting . . . wait! You don't have to run with them to get a picture, do you?"

He chuckled. "No. The bulls run for a week. I will be on the sidelines and balconies. I will have a different location every day."

"My goodness."

"So, Lauren, I have been doing all the talking. Please tell me. What brings you to Paris?"

"My aunt died, and I need to settle her estate." She took a bite and set her bread down. A tiny piece of tapenade remained on her lower lip. He wanted to lick it off.

He didn't often have romantic thoughts about a woman he'd only just met, and for an unknown reason the images stole his attention. He needed to calm his breathing and regain control.

"I'm sorry to hear about your aunt."

She licked her bottom lip, and Andre shifted in his chair. "Thank you. I didn't know her very well. She moved to Paris when I was young, and we didn't get to see her very much."

"We?"

"Oh, yes. My brother and I. He stayed back in New York while I handle things here."

"Where are your parents?"

She blinked and looked down. *Merde!* "Um, they died in a car accident over twenty years ago."

He leaned forward and reached his hand to cover hers. "I'm so sorry, Lauren. I'm sorry I asked."

"No. It's okay. It was a long time ago," she gave him a small smile.

He knew she was being polite. He had a sense that the emotion ran deep on that topic. How could it not?

"So you are traveling alone?" The thought both concerned and excited him.

"Yes. The attorney expects I'll be here for about four weeks. My biggest project is clearing out my aunt's house and selling it."

"I see."

"This is a day off, so to speak. Tomorrow, I return to my aunt's house and start to sort through her belongings. The sooner I get through that, the sooner the house can go on the market."

"Do you think you will get other days off like this?" He knew he had to see her again.

She smiled a beautiful shy smile. "Yes, I think I will."

"Do you have plans for the rest of the day? Would you consider letting me show you around to some of the monuments and attractions around the City of Lights." *Also known as the City of Love.*

She smiled back at him. "Yes, I'd like that."

Andre and Lauren meandered through the city some more. He pointed out significant sights, and a few minor ones relating to his college years. She could listen to him talk all day. She loved his accent. He cupped his hand around hers, and she didn't stop him. How could she when it felt so positively good?

He took her to the *Arc de Triomphe*, bought them tickets, and they went to the top. Of course, it wasn't nearly as tall as the Eiffel Tower, so she felt completely at ease.

After some time, she turned to him.

"It's getting a bit late for me. I need to be up early to go to my aunt's house. I should get back to my hotel."

"Of course. May I walk you?"

"Yes, thank you." She told him where she was staying, knowing it was close. All Lauren could think was how utterly at ease she felt with Andre. She found herself intrigued by him. He looked to be about thirty-five. Did he have a girlfriend? Surely not, if he was spending all this time with her. Walking hand-in-hand, no less.

What was she thinking?

She was here for only four weeks. She needed to get her business done and get home.

They arrived outside the hotel, and she stopped to look up at him.

"Thank you so much for lunch and for . . . helping me on the Eiffel Tower. I had no idea my fear of heights was so severe." She smirked.

"Lauren, may I take you to dinner tomorrow night?" He took hold of her other hand. His eyes smiling.

How could she say no to that handsome face? *"Oui."*

His eyes twinkled. He flashed his beautiful teeth, and the sight of his dimple made her smile back.

His smile faded as he placed a finger under her chin and lifted it slightly. He leaned down and gave her a slow, easy kiss with his soft lips. Heavenly. She lifted her hands and rested them on his warm chest.

He glossed his lips over hers and dragged his tongue slowly over her lower lip. She separated her lips, and his tongue slipped inside. She tilted her head for more and found herself leaning into his solid body.

His hands moved to cup the sides of her head as he took the kiss deeper. His tongue sinuously stroked along hers. *Oh, what a mouth.* Their delicious kiss simply stole her breath. The kiss went on for several moments—long and hot—causing her sex to begin to ache.

He slowly tapered off until he pulled his lips away.

"*Mon Dieu*," he breathed against her forehead. "Tomorrow. Dinner. How is seven o'clock?"

"Good." She breathed into his neck.

He kissed her forehead and brought his hands down. "Good night, *Mademoiselle* Lauren. I'll see you tomorrow," he reached for her hand and kissed her knuckles. He made eye contact one last time before he spun around to head back up the sidewalk.

She exhaled and sighed. *What a kiss.* She was grateful he put a stop to that kiss because she was quite certain she was incapable of doing it herself.

What on earth was he thinking? He kissed her! Andre was so taken with the beautiful Lauren, he simply couldn't stop for wanting to touch her lips, taste her. Her glowing face, pretty pink lips and exquisitely shapely body beckoned to him. He gritted his teeth. His better logic told him to leave her alone. The impulsive side howled for him to kiss her.

And now he'd made another date with her. *What was he getting himself into?*

CHAPTER FOUR

MR. BERNARD confirmed that he would have his driver outside her hotel the following morning to drive her to the house. He had offered to hire help to sort and box her aunt's belongings, which she declined. Lauren knew the two previous days had merely given her a glimpse of what lay at her aunt's house. Above anything else, she needed to assess what was under that roof before making any hasty decisions.

Mr. Bernard also informed her that five days from now, her aunt's memorial service would take place. Lauren made a note, and needed think about that later.

When she arrived at her aunt's house, she reviewed her progress in the kitchen. Almost everything was boxed. *Check.*

Next, she would work on the living room. Aside from a new wall color, the room didn't require much. She grabbed some framed photos she saw on the shelves and drawers, and boxed them. She noticed one of her parents, and smiled.

Afterward, she stuck blue tape where the helpers could come in and box items for donation. She also marked two pieces to be removed and create more space, but essentially that room was complete.

The dining room and powder room were easier. But the office was another matter. The floor-to-ceiling bookcases were chock-full of photos, books, mementos, and figurines. The desk and credenza had more of the same. She let out a breath, deciding to tackle that room later.

She broke for lunch and shot a quick email to Cole to give him an update. She hadn't thought about the spa all day. Interesting. Hopefully, things were running smoothly.

After lunch, Lauren took a deep breath and entered the office. *Where to start?* Bookshelves held a few dozen books, quite a few mementos from her aunt's travels and more pictures. *Oh dear.* She licked her lips. There were more pictures of her mother and father. One from their wedding, a few of her mom during pregnancy, and of course, some of Lauren and Cole as babies.

Lauren blinked rapidly. She grabbed them and wrapped them in paper before shoving them into a cardboard box.

She continued to scan the shelves for photos. She quickly caught sight of her aunt wearing a helmet and goggles, with her arms stretched wide with a smile almost as wide. Clearly that was her foray into skydiving. Boy, it looked like she had a blast. There were more pictures of a similar vein. Some at parties with friends, some skiing, one snorkeling, and—what?—was that the *top* of the Sydney Harbour Bridge? *Unbelievable!* Her aunt was a true daredevil.

Lauren grabbed the photos and stacked them in the cardboard box. She proceeded to the closed part of the bookcase. She opened the doors and nothing could prepare her for what she saw. Book after book of photos. *Oh dear Lord.* Her heart thundered in her chest. This is too personal, she thought. The books seemed to stare at her as she stared back.

She rolled her shoulders back, slipped off her shoes and sat down in front of the cabinet. She wasn't exactly sure why she felt compelled to go through the photos. What she'd expect to do with the books, she didn't know.

The first book seemed to be a recent one. Many actions shots, more pictures of friends at parties, several appeared to be at the house. Celebrations and trips. There were a few pages with a gentleman— smiling, holding hands, kissing. He seemed quite smitten with Aunt Rosie.

The next book had more of the same, but based on the fashions and hair styles, Lauren was going backward chronologically. Perhaps at the memorial service, her friends would like to see these. It would certainly show how much they all meant to Rosie.

Then sure as the sun sets, Lauren got to an album with pictures of her parents. She couldn't put it down even if the house were on fire. She took a deep breath and turned the pages. Her parents with her grandparents, at their house, on vacation. Maybe Mom sent these pictures to Aunt Rosie while she was in Paris.

She sighed at the pictures of the four of them—mom, dad, herself, and Cole. They looked so happy. One showed them swimming in the hotel pool during a trip to the Pocono Mountains. That was a fun trip.

She flipped the page and gasped. Larger than life, a picture of her parents arm-in-arm kissing. Another with her father as he stood behind her mother, his arms wrapped around her waist. Their faces aglow. Lauren hadn't seen any of these pictures before.

Surely, there were photos at their house growing up. Her brows came together. Where were those? Her aunt and uncle must have scooped them up before Lauren and Cole could see them.

Tears formed in her eyes as Lauren continued her perusal. So many pictures of her family. Happy times documented in old photographs. God, how she missed her parents. She couldn't hold it in anymore. A sob escaped, and the flood waters broke loose.

Dear God, help her get through this. The tears ran down her cheeks. She wiped them with the back of her hand. She needed tissues or she would ruin the photos.

She didn't remember any of those photos, but she remembered most of the trips and the places where they were taken. She gleaned several of Cole as a baby. Mom held Cole while Lauren went down a slide. Another one with Dad pushing her on a swing.

Further back, Mom was pregnant with her, smiling for the camera, her head tilted. She must have been nine months because she held her hands over her big belly. Another—oh God—her father squatted down and kissed her mother's belly.

Lauren couldn't take anymore. She slammed the book shut and pushed it off her lap. She covered her face and lay down on the rug and bawled. She sobbed unceasingly. She felt a lump in her throat and her stomach was queasy.

She missed her parents. They should be here. They should be doing this for Aunt Rosie. She wasn't strong enough to do this alone. Why did they go so soon? She needed them. She needed them now. It was so unfair.

The emotion felt so raw, as if it were new, not from twenty-three years ago.

She needed to stop this now. She called the driver to pick her up. Next, she texted Mr. Bernard to ask for help for the next day. The sooner she got the place packed, the better.

Lauren rinsed off her face in the powder room, slipped on her sunglasses, locked the front door, and stepped into the back of the awaiting car.

"My hotel, please," was all she could get out.

When she made it up to her room, she slipped off her shoes and collapsed onto the bed. She was so drained she couldn't even cry anymore. She stared into nothingness until finally she closed her eyes and sleep overtook her.

CHAPTER FIVE

THE NEXT THING she knew, her hotel phone rang. Loudly. *Geez!* She swung her legs around and placed her feet on the floor.

"Hello?" She sounded groggy.

"Lauren? Is that you?"

"Oh, Andre. I'm sorry. What time is it?"

"Seven-ten. Lauren, are you alright?"

"No, not really," she grumbled.

"What's your room number? I'm coming up." He sounded serious. She gave him the number—thank God it was on the phone—because she didn't have the cognition to tell him she'd have to take a rain check.

He knocked at the door barely two minutes later. Oh, she must look like hell. She smoothed her hair with both hands and opened the door for him.

He took one look at her, stepped inside, and asked, "What happened?"

"I found books, photo albums, of my parents." She dropped her head and shook it twice. "I just couldn't take it anymore."

A sob slipped passed her lips, and she immediately covered her face with her hands. She knew her crying over her parents was not a pretty sight. Far from it.

Andre quickly stepped closer and circled his arms around her in an embrace. God, he felt so good. His warmth enveloped her. She sobbed again and her knees felt weak. She started to crumble and he instantly scooped her legs under an arm and carried her to the bed. He sat on the bed with her on his lap.

"Tell me. What did you see?"

"Oh God, Andre. So many pictures of my parents." She pulled her head up and wiped her eyes with her fingertips. "They looked so happy. We were all so happy. I thought I had mourned this and would be fine after twenty years, but it hit me like a ton of bricks. I couldn't finish. I had to go."

"Of course." He kissed her forehead.

"There were just so many photos, some places I remember, but I hardly remember them being taken." A sob escaped. "God, I miss them so much." And a new wave of tears streamed down her cheeks.

He kissed her forehead again, and brought her back in close to him. She grasped her arms around his neck and cried for several moments. She cried until she felt cried-out.

Finally, she lifted her head. Why was it she poured her heart out to someone she only just met? Was she really that comfortable with him or just desperate being in a foreign country, battling old wounds, alone?

She raised her head, and her sight traveled to his shirt. His poor shirt—wet with all her tears.

"I'm so sorry about your shirt."

"Shh. Don't worry about that. Do you feel better?" His brow knit together as he searched her eyes for reassurance.

"Yes."

"Are you hungry?"

"Yes, but I'm sorry, Andre. I can't go out tonight."

"Of course not. Let me call for room service."

She paused. She needed to eat, and since Andre had already seen her at her worst, where was the harm is letting him stay?

"Okay. I will have some pasta. Spaghetti always makes me feel better, at least a little."

"Yes, comfort food," he grinned at her.

"I need to take a shower. Is that alright?"

"Of course. When you are finished, the food should be ready."

And with that she nodded and headed for the bathroom. As the water ran, she could hear him on the phone. She glanced at her reflection in the mirror and clipped her hair up. Well, the good news was her mascara wasn't down to her cheeks because she had cried that away earlier. Now she was left with blotchy skin and puffy eyes. Lovely.

The hot shower did wonderful things for her. The tension eased from her muscles while the water pummeled her shoulders. Those were particularly tight.

In New York, that wouldn't be a problem. She'd just put herself on the schedule as the last appointment of the day and let Margie work those muscles back to happy and relaxed. Perhaps she should find a spa here.

Not wanting to put her other clothes back on, she slipped on the super fluffy, white robe and stepped out of the bathroom. She strolled into the main room and saw Andre arranging the dinner plates on the table.

He tilted his head to face her and smiled. He lifted the cover off her entrée. "Spaghetti and meatballs. Plus there is some salad with vinaigrette dressing. And a *chocolat* dessert. Do you like *chocolat*?"

She smiled a shy smile. "Yes, very much."

"Please sit." He motioned his arm toward the chair at the round table.

She took a seat and dug into her salad first. "What did you order?"

"I'm having lamb."

They ate in silence, mostly because Lauren suspected he was as hungry as she. She realized how totally different this night was from what he might have planned. Damn.

"Andre?"

He looked over at her. "Yes."

"I'm sorry about how this evening has gone. About ruining your dinner plans."

His eyes trained on her, he set his fork down and said, "No need to apologize. I am glad to be here with you. We can do dinner out another time. I'm certainly happy to offer my shoulder to you during your time of need. Lauren, I like your company, wherever we are." His eyes appeared so sincere even as his lips gave a slight smile.

She smiled and nodded. His face seemed so filled with honesty and trustworthiness. It was as though he could reach her soul, touch her heart. "Andre, where are your parents?"

"They live in Bordeaux, in the south of France. They are mostly retired." He leaned over with the bottle of red wine to refill her glass.

"Do you have any brothers or sisters?"

"*Oui*, one sister. She is married and lives in London with her husband."

"Do you get to see your family?"

"I saw my parents last month, and my sister was here visiting a few months ago. I will go see her . . ." He looked up for a brief moment. "In August."

She felt full, so she covered her plate and placed it on the rolling cart.

"Would you like *chocolat* mousse?" he asked, his head cocked to the side.

"I think I'll pass. Maybe I'll have it later." Out of the blue, a huge yawn overtook her. "I'm full and I'm getting tired."

His lips curved watching her. "I can see that."

He wiped his mouth with the napkin, covered his empty plate and placed it on the cart. He rose, and she did too. "I'll bid you a good night. Perhaps we can have dinner tomorrow night," he stopped suddenly, "but there is no pressure."

She kept his gaze. "I would like that."

She smoothed her lips together. Today had to be the worst of it. Surely, tomorrow would be better, and she wouldn't spoil a date with her handsome Frenchman.

He leaned down to kiss her closed mouth, and said softly, "Goodnight, Lauren."

Her heart gave a little patter. He must have felt it too, because he only stood upright, still in her personal space.

"I should go," he said without moving a muscle.

She nodded and reached her hands to his chest. She smoothed her palms over his cotton shirt, over his wonderful chest muscles. She should stop touching him, or he'll never be able to leave. But she couldn't.

"I find that I don't know how to say goodnight to you, Andre. I know that sounds foolish."

"I know what you mean." He rested his hands on her hips, letting her think about what she wanted.

She slid her warm, delicate hands over his chest, and stopped at a button. Her gaze rose to his. "Andre, I need to ask for forgiveness. I don't want you to go, but with the emotional rollercoaster of a day I'm having, I fear I might start something I cannot finish."

"I am a big boy, Lauren. I can handle it."

Her pink lips raised into a sweet smile. With a lick of her lips, she slipped the button of his shirt. She unbuttoned another and another and stopped when she reached his waistline.

Her breath grew slightly louder, or maybe that was his.

Her slim fingers slipped over his bare chest under his shirt and pushed it out of the way. Her eyelids drooped slightly as she moved closer to kiss his chest. Slowly, she kissed his collarbone, his pectorals, and on her toes, she kissed his neck while clutching his chest.

He moaned. Her movements were slow, as if fascinated by her exploration. He commanded himself to be patient and wait for her lead. After the emotional and exhausting day she'd had, the fact she was interested in more than a handshake completely floored him.

"You smell good," she breathed into his neck as she continued to kiss, lick and nibble at his neck.

Mon Dieu, help him not rip open that robe, knowing full well she wore nothing underneath. As much as she wanted tonight, he would give. There was no rush.

"Andre?"

"*Oui.*"

"Would you kiss me again like you did yesterday?" she peered up at him through her lashes.

Did she need to ask?

He stroked his hands up her arms, over her shoulders and neck to her beautiful face. Gently his lips caressed hers, and she didn't hesitate to open her mouth to his. His tongue dipped into her mouth to find hers waiting. Her tongue played against his, and with every stroke, his cock swelled.

In an unexpected move, without breaking their kiss, Lauren eased her robe open enough to lay her tantalizing breasts against his bare chest. His breath quivered, and her flesh trembled against his.

Mon Dieu. He must maintain control.

She moaned. A waft of aromatic Lauren-scent filled his nostrils. His balls positively ached.

She drew back a millimeter. "Don't stop kissing me, please. I love how you kiss me," she breathed over his mouth.

He moaned his response. He wouldn't stop kissing her for all the gold in *Banque de France.*

He desperately wanted to run his hands over her naked body. He decided to test her comfort level. He slid his hands down her neck, across her chest to her lush, swollen breasts. His thumbs skated over her long, perky nipples.

She whimpered. *Bonne.* He continued his fondling and entranced by her moans and whimpers he almost didn't feel her leg rise and hook around his ass.

She gingerly writhed against him. Her hands gripped his shoulders tightly as she pushed her body close to his.

Instinctively, he held her naked thigh firmly against his hip and bent his knees to align his aching cock against her delicious sex. He restrained from glancing down at her femininity just yet. Only when he felt himself over her sex did he rock against her.

"Ah," she groaned.

He did it again.

She moaned louder and pulled her lips off his to take in air.

He pinched her nipple one last time and moved his free hand to cup her ass and hold her tightly to his cock. He hoped his pants wouldn't abrade her too harshly, but he didn't want to stop riding hard against her sweetness.

"Lean back, *ma chérie.* I've got you."

Without hesitation, she arched her body, let go of his shoulders, and placed her hands on the table. The clank of her hairclip hitting the table did nothing to interrupt their lust. Her robe slipped off her shoulders leaving her breasts on display for a willing mouth. She moved her hips with his gyrations, and he brought his mouth down to cover one delicious nipple.

"Andre," she panted, "please . . . don't stop."

He glanced down at her lovely pussy. He couldn't feel it through his pants, but she kept her silky mons. Oh *Jésus*!

She kept herself trimmed. He loved looking at her brown wisps and how it glistened with her moisture.

Her moans increased, and he knew she was close, which was good. He gritted his teeth as his balls tightened in anticipation.

Then she let out a low, but long, cry and her head tossed from the right to the left. He let loose as well, not caring that his semen would soak his underpants, and probably more. He groaned, kissed her breast again, and kissed up to her mouth as he brought her upright.

She snaked her arms around his neck and dropped her head into his neck and breathed heavily. He slowly released her leg and smoothed her robe down.

"Andre, I don't know what came over me." She breathed audibly and pulled back to look at his trousers. "Oh no. Your pants are ruined."

He cupped her chin and brought her gaze to his. "No. It will clean easily. I love what just happened. I hope you don't feel awkward, because I don't." Before she could protest, he claimed her mouth with his. Her perfect mouth and exquisite tongue coaxed and caressed his for several long moments.

She moaned into his mouth.

As much as he wanted to stay, he knew she needed rest. He broke the kiss and said, "I should clean up a little before I go out in public." He grinned down at her.

She smiled and nodded. "Help yourself," she said as she waved an arm toward the bathroom.

He strode back out of the bathroom, shirt untucked, and stood by the door. She met him and immediately went into his arms. He kissed her forehead.

She pulled back. "This is my cell phone number," she gave him a piece of paper.

He would love nothing more than to see her again. "Dinner tomorrow?"

"*Magnifique*," she whispered.

He loved to hear her little bits of French. He kissed the tops of her knuckles and caressed her cheek with his hand. He leaned down and gave her one last goodbye kiss before ducking out the door.

What came over her, she may never know. She should be burning up with embarrassment over that come-on. She was vulnerable, not herself. Clearly she'd been clouded with grief, because the Lauren she knew didn't throw herself at a man. She shook her head. *What were you thinking?*

She lifted her fingertips to her lips tender from the kissing. One thing was true, this affair was going to be earth-shattering. She shuddered, and laughed despite herself.

CHAPTER SIX

THE TWO HELPERS arrived at her aunt's house right after Lauren. They both knew some English, but clearly had already gotten instructions from Mr. Bernard. Excellent.

They powered through the house, clearing, boxing, and organizing. Lauren assessed what maintenance needed to be done in each room.

She recognized that she felt very different. There was a calm in her that wasn't there before. She didn't feel so emotional or bleak. As embarrassing as it might have been, crying on Andre's shoulder had been amazingly cathartic.

At five o'clock, she called Mr. Bernard with an update. Painters were expected first thing the next morning. The landscapers would arrive a few hours after. Lauren was grateful the estate had budgeted to pay for all these expenses.

She mentally planned her next two days; getting everything ready for pictures on Tuesday seemed very feasible. *Oh dear, Monday.* That was to be her aunt's memorial service. She had better plan what she was going to say. She sighed aloud.

Andre called her cell shortly after she returned to her hotel room.

"*Bonjour*, Lauren. How did everything go today? How are you feeling?"

"I feel good. Thank you. I can tell you all about it when we meet." *Oh, was that too presumptuous?*

"*Bonne*. How would you feel if I made you dinner tonight at my place?"

She smiled at the thought. "I would like that."

"I will pick you up in an hour then. Is that okay?"

"Perfect," she hung up and skipped to the bathroom to run her bath. She would have time for a little soak before she needed to be downstairs.

Andre stepped out of his car and toward a very beautiful Lauren waiting in front of her hotel. Her black skirt hugged her curves. He planted a kiss on her smiling pink lips.

"*Bonsoir*."

"Good evening," she replied with an adorable smile on her face.

"You look lovely." He loved her smell.

"Thank you." Her lips curved sweetly.

"Ready to go?"

She nodded. "Yes."

He opened her car door, and placed her bag in the trunk of his Smart car. Then he strolled around to the driver's side and climbed in.

"Andre, what kind of a car is this?"

"A Smart car." He glanced over at her.

"There's no back seat."

"*Oui.*"

"For such a tall man, it is really hard for me to picture you in a little car like this."

He could see the twinkle in her eyes. *Was she holding back a laugh?*

He reached his hand over to her thigh, stroked down to several centimeters above her knee and squeezed.

"Ah," she yelped and jumped off the seat. She giggled.

"I'll have you know, *mademoiselle*, this car gets excellent gas mileage, which is key in Europe since the gas prices are so exorbitant. Additionally, because I travel so much, I'm rarely driving it."

She bit her lip and seemed to hold back a smile. "Yes, it is such a wise purchase. You are a wise man indeed."

He harrumphed and continued driving.

The drive took only fifteen minutes, and it was all he could do to focus on the road and not on Lauren. She sat beside him in a black straight skirt, legs crossed. Long, lean, silky legs. She wore a pale pink cashmere sweater that showed a peek of her cleavage. Beautiful.

They parked in front of his building, and he held open her door for her. They walked up the stairs to his second story apartment. As he unlocked his door, a little summer wind gust blew through the breezeway, catching them by surprise. Her wavy, light brown locks flew across her face. He straightened, and with an index finger he stroked her hair off her face.

He felt a tiny shiver as his finger trailed down her throat. "Thank you," she whispered.

He smiled down at her.

He opened the door and stretched out his arm. "After you."

Her eyes danced around the place before turning back to him. "Andre, this is a great apartment."

"Thank you. My sister helped me decorate after I got the place."

She strolled in and set her purse on a chair in the living room, sliding her hand over the smooth leather. He went to the kitchen and watched as she looked at the books and pictures on his tables and shelves. She held up a framed photo, and called to him, "Is this your sister?"

"*Oui*. Do you like seafood?"

"Yes." She set the photo back down and walked to the kitchen. "What are you making?"

"*Bouillabaisse*." He watched as her eyes lit up.

"Oh, yum. Can I help with anything?"

"Yes, please open the wine in the refrigerator. Glasses are in that cabinet," he said as he motioned with his chin.

They set the table with glasses, bowls, silverware and a fresh baguette. He carefully set a large bowl in the middle of the table and served her.

She took a seat across from him at his square table. It wasn't large, but it was perfect for intimate dinners like this.

At her first bite, he watched as her eyes closed, and her lips press together. "Mmm." He heard the little mewl from her sweet lips and felt his heart swell.

"You like?"

"I love." She opened her eyes and smiled.

He took one bite and smiled himself, pleased with his efforts. "So, how did things go at your aunt's house today?"

She blotted her mouth and looked thoughtfully at the table, then lifted her head to face him. "It went really well. I could almost feel a lightness that I hadn't felt before. As much I don't want to admit it, my embarrassing bawling session yesterday seemed to be very cathartic and healing. You know what I mean?"

He nodded. "I am glad to hear that, and please don't feel embarrassed."

She tilted her head and smiled.

"So when can you put it on the market?" he asked.

"I will have the rest of my aunt's things sent out for donation or to storage tomorrow. The painters will come out," she ripped off a hunk of baguette, "and the landscapers too. The house should be ready for listing by Tuesday. When do you leave for Greenland?"

"Monday."

"Hmm."

He paused and held his spoon still. "What?"

"Monday is my aunt's memorial service."

He let go of the spoon, and a tiny clink sounded as it hit the ceramic bowl. He reached over and took a hold of her hand.

"Oh, Lauren. I'm so sorry I cannot be here for you."

The corners of her lips rose. "Thank you, but I'll be okay. I am going into this with eyes open. It helps that this is mostly for her friends. I wasn't very close to her."

"So she never had children?"

Lauren shook her head.

"She never got married?"

She shook her head again.

"Wow."

"I learned something, Andre. I am grateful for what you did yesterday, and I don't want to diminish that, but dealing with all of this has taught me so much about myself." She sat a little taller. "I'm confident I can handle Monday," she smiled.

He held her gaze. "You can."

They cleaned up afterward in the kitchen, working easily side by side. He poured them both more wine and asked, "Would you like to watch a movie?"

Her mouth gaped, and then closed. She tipped her head and said, "I don't think I'll understand any of what they're saying."

He grinned at her. "We can watch an English movie. We get television stations from the UK."

Her eyes rounded. "Oh, that's right. Sure, let's watch a movie."

As she made herself comfortable, he dimmed most of the lights, reached for the remote and the set came to life. He flipped for a while, passing mostly French and news stations, and he stopped on an English station. She recognized the movie immediately—Titanic.

"I love this movie." She'd only seen it about twenty-five times.

He placed the remote on the cocktail table and glanced at her. "How many times have you seen it?"

She tried to keep a straight face. "Once or twice."

"Hmm."

Andre leaned back and stretched his arm over the back of the sofa. Lauren nearly sighed aloud when she felt his body heat radiate to her shoulders and neck.

It only took Lauren about two seconds to realize where they were in the movie. *Oh dear.*

She must have murmured something because Andre turned toward her and asked, "Excuse me?"

"Hmm? Nothing."

The scene was right before Jack and Rose made love. It had to be one of her favorites. Touching, but hot and steamy at the same time.

Without moving her head, she glanced at Andre from the corner of her eye. He watched every move on the screen.

She worried that he might hear her breathing. It wasn't the characters on the screen, as much as the idea of what they were doing, and how she and Andre could do those same things. She smoothed her lips between her teeth and willed her heart to slow down.

Andre's thumb slipped under her hair and began stroking up and down her neck. Electrified little tingles shot throughout her body. She resisted closing her eyes.

After several moments, the scene before them finished. Andre spoke to her without moving his head, "Well, you know what I think?"

"What?" she looked his way.

He met her gaze. "We can do better than that."

She swallowed hard. "Really? Because that seemed pretty hot."

He gave her a half-smirk and shrugged a shoulder.

She narrowed her eyes. "Show me."

He lowered his hand, leaned forward and pressed the mute on the remote.

"My pleasure."

He bent down, grazed his fingertips over her calf as he raised her leg and slipped off her pump. He did the same for the other foot. Shivers shot up her legs. With both hands, he lifted her legs onto his lap and gently pulled her closer so that her behind bumped up to his thigh.

He returned his arm to the back of the sofa and caressed her neck with his long, strong fingers. Lauren fought a moan. He rested his other hand on her knee.

"Like right here." His thumb ran circles just under her ear. Her body quivered, and her nipples peaked. "This can be a very erotic area for a woman."

He leaned in and kissed where his thumb had been. Slowly his lips roamed her entire throat, leaving a hot trail in its wake. She caught the masculine scent of his shampoo. With his every move, she grew damp with desire.

He brought his hands to her waist and slowly caressed her skin under her sweater. He inched the sweater higher and helped her take it off.

"And of course here," he dragged a finger through her cleavage and along her bra-line. "Touches in this area can be rather arousing." He leaned in for a sensual, slow kiss, and breathed against her lips. "What do you think?"

She sighed as Andre continued to kiss and caress her. As his finger stroked her skin under the lace of bra, he went higher and slipped the bra straps off her shoulders. Her bra fell down and revealed bits of areola.

She leaned closer to him and her hands traveled, one to his head and the other to his knee.

His kiss traveled her face, her throat, and without stopping, his fingers flipped open the front clasp of her bra. He immediately caught one breast in his large warm hand. She moaned, and let her eyes close, and her head drop back.

Both hands came to cup her breasts, massaging and kneading the flesh as his lips closed in over one very taut nipple.

Her fingers wove through his dark brown hair, keeping him right where she wanted him.

"Andre," she panted.

"Lie back, *ma chérie*."

She did as he bid and almost regretted it because his lips were no longer on her.

His hands slid down her torso, over her skirt and slowly skimmed under her skirt, up her thighs. His heated eyes trained on her.

"Tell me, do you like being touched right here?" His fingertips glossed over her damp panties under her skirt.

She joggled at his slightest touch. "Uh."

"Ah, *oui*. I think perhaps you do." He eased one finger under her thong and ran it along her lips. She tried to separate her legs to give him more access, but her skirt was too tight.

"Would you like to take off this skirt?"

She nodded. "Yes."

He took a hold of one of her hands, and as he stood, he raised her to sit.

She was certain he expected her to stand, but in this position, she was inches from the hard bulge in the front of his pants. She forgot about her skirt.

She skimmed her tongue over her bottom lip. Next, she flung her bra and brought her two hands smoothly over his thighs up to his cock. His lips parted and he looked down to watch her move.

She worked his belt, the pants' button, and slowly slid his zipper down. She grabbed a hold of his waistband and tugged his pants and briefs down his thighs.

She gasped. What a beautiful sight. She held him gently, and with her thumb she smoothed the drop of moisture that shone on the tip. She wetted her lips with her tongue and leaned forward to swipe it across the head.

"Mmm," she smiled.

She brought her lips fully over him and closed on his head completely. He groaned and gripped the back of her head. She moved her mouth down his shaft and sucked gently. Slowly she increased the pressure, and his hips gave an involuntary jolt.

"Mmm," she moaned against his member.

"*Chérie*. No more," he panted. "No more." He pulled out and she peered up at him. Knowing he would come if she continued felt so powerful, heady.

"You wicked woman," he said with an amused smile on his lips. He grabbed both her hands and yanked her up to stand, and into his arms. He crashed his lips on hers. His kiss was urgent as his tongue thrust deeply into her mouth.

His hands unfastened her skirt at the back and sent it to the floor. He broke the kiss, a wicked glint in his eyes.

"Let's see what else you like. Sit."

She glanced back and landed on the sofa facing him. She sat nearly naked and watched as he shed his clothes. He pushed the cocktail table away and knelt in between her legs. He held on to her thighs and caressed them. He leaned over her and fastened his mouth to hers. She grasped his head. His fingers tantalized her as they smoothed over her panties. His every move, every touch, flamed her blood.

"Andre." Overwhelming need consumed her.

He dove his fingers beneath her thong and played with her sex. He distracted her with his addicting kisses when she heard the subtle rip of her panties. He pulled the fabric from underneath her and tossed her thong to the ground.

"This first one will be fast, *chérie*," he said as he pushed her thighs wide, almost to the point of pain and plunged the flat of his tongue over her clit, grinding against it.

She jolted, arched her back and shuddered. His expert movements had her panting and, in mere moments, she cried out in a wave of shimmering joy. He played his tongue on her for as long as she trembled. Finally, she went limp and gasped for air. He licked gently around her sex and poked his tongue inside. She held his head and attempted to push him back as the sensation was so strong.

He continued his pleasurable ministrations with his tongue when he took two fingers and pushed into her soaking channel.

"Ah," she moaned.

The stimulation from his tongue mixed with the twisting strokes of his fingers made her flesh quiver. Oh, God, the sensation was insanely good. *How does he do that?*

"Oh." Her hands clung to his head, and her hips shamelessly pulsed against his lips.

Her inner muscles tightened. Andre pulled back, and she almost screamed. He retrieved a condom from his pants pocket and slipped it on. He held her hands and said, "Come here." He simply fell backward and brought her on top of him.

Skin to skin. He felt so good—toned chest and broad shoulders. *Yummy.*

"You have to do this, *chérie*. I do not trust myself."

She licked her lips and sat up, and pushed herself higher on her knees. She held him and aligned herself while Andre held onto her hips. Slowly, she lowered herself down on him until fully sheathed inside her. They both let out long, low moans.

For a moment, she couldn't move. She savored the exquisite feeling of having him inside her. It was as if he was made for her.

She laid her hands on his chest, pulsing over him, her hair falling around his face. His hands framed her face and brought her lips to his. His tongue pushed inside, sliding sensuously against hers.

They moved together, sharing body heat and air to breathe. So close. He seemed to sense the achy need in her and reached between them to graze his thumb over her hot button. Pushing against his chest, she sat upright and arched against his hand. He flexed in time with her movements.

She increased the speed while he increased the pressure on her clit.

"Ah," she breathed. Her climax built until the release streaked up her body, and she called out.

Andre held on to her hips, thrust harder and came audibly, his eyelids falling closed. She curled down over him and huffed into his neck.

"Oh my God," she panted.

"*Oui*," he wrapped his arms around her and kissed her hair. "You are *magnifique*."

CHAPTER SEVEN

LAUREN AWOKE WITH a smile on her face. Andre drove her back to her hotel the night before and gave her one of his sensuous, lingering kisses. She wanted to lounge in bed naked all day and call Andre to come over, but she had too much to do.

Mr. Bernard's driver picked Lauren up early, and she arrived to find the painters unloading their truck.

Lauren reviewed her plan with the foreman who spoke decent English and left them to their work. The two helpers arrived later and loaded the last few boxes of photos to go into storage. They also brought cleaning supplies, so within an hour Lauren donned rubber gloves to scrub countertops, floors, and toilets. She cleaned for hours what she could, knowing the painters would be working through Monday.

If everything went as planned, the house would be ready for the real estate agent to take pictures on Tuesday. Lauren stood and stretched out her back. She felt confident the house could be ready by then.

She walked outside to check on the landscaping progress and was pleasantly surprised. Bushes were neatly trimmed, new flowers were being planted, and the grass was cut.

With a quick peek at her watch she decided to place a call to Cole and see how things were going in New York.

"Hello?"

"Cole? It's Lauren."

"Hey, Lauren. I'm about to go in an elevator. If I drop you, I'll call you back."

"Okay. So how's it going?"

"Good. How about you? How's everything going in Paris?"

"Fabulous. At first I was overwhelmed, but I'm getting in a groove. I'm making progress on the house, a room at a time. Cole, she has a ton of photo books," her voice dropped an octave. "I'll bring them back. You may like to look at them."

"Yeah. That would be good. So what's going on now?"

"Painters and landscapers are here now. I've got help to do some cleaning. And the real estate agent plans to put the house on the market Tuesday."

"How are things otherwise in Paris? Your photos from the Eiffel Tower were awesome. Who took them?"

"Well, this is a great city—so much to see and do. I hope I can take more of it in before I have to leave. And to answer your question, the person that took those pictures is a photographer. His name is Andre." Her voice softened at just mention of his name.

"Ah. So are you and Andre going out?"

"We have, yes. And we probably will again."

"Well, be careful, would you?" She recognized that concern in his voice.

"I will. I better go," she said.

"Okay, take care. I'll talk to you soon."

"Love you."

"Love you back," and she disconnected the line.

Next, she dialed the driver for a ride back to the hotel and, if she was lucky, the chance to see Andre.

She felt flutters inside thinking of him. What he did to her, how he made her feel, was astronomical. As she gathered her things, she briefly wondered how many girlfriends he had in the past. Don't think about that, she told herself. *Enjoy the time you have together now*.

***

Andre dialed Lauren's cell and tapped his foot anxiously. He knew she was working hard, so he didn't want to bother her. But *Mon Dieu*, she invaded his thoughts all day.

"Hello, Andre."

"*Allô, chérie*. Care to go out to dinner with me tonight?"

"Andre, you're spoiling me." He could practically hear her smile.

"*Oui*. That is my job. You are the guest in my country. It is important for you to feel welcome, comfortable, . . . and pleasured."

He heard her breath hitch. "Really?" she asked in a sing-songy way.

"Ah, *oui*. So what time shall I pick you up? I do not want to be neglectful in my duties."

She giggled. What a lovely sound. "How about one hour?"

"Okay. I will see you in one hour," he hung up the phone.

Andre greeted Lauren in front of her hotel again. Yet, this time, the kiss wasn't short. He missed her, and after their deep heated kiss, she'd know it.

"Oh my. What was that for?" she smiled at him.

In heels, she stood closer to his height, and he loved how her body could so easily nestle into his. *Merde!* He needed to keep his focus. What had come over him? A woman had never affected him like this before.

"You look beautiful. I hope you had a great day."

"I did. Thank you."

"The restaurant I want to go to is close. Can you walk a few blocks?"

"Of course," she smiled at him.

They walked hand in hand along the sidewalks of a calm, balmy Paris evening. Occasionally, a breeze would ruffle her hair. Some areas of sidewalk were cobblestone, and Andre took it slow so she wouldn't catch her heels. Twinkling lights from the near-by shops showed. Lauren glanced up to see the moon softly aglow which added to the romance, even though it wasn't dark yet.

"Lauren, do you have to go to the house tomorrow?"

"No, not really."

"How would you like to go for a drive to the wine country?"

Her heart leaped. This would be a huge thing. She had crossed so many lines with Andre, particularly sleeping with him so soon. She'd always waited several dates before she even considered sleeping with a guy. Now, he wanted to go away with her. It wasn't a question of trust really. She bit her lip.

"Um. Would we return to Paris tomorrow night, or spend the night there?"

He looked at her, his tongue darted out to wet his lips. "I thought we would stay at a little chateau, but we can certainly drive home at night if you prefer."

Oh, that sounds nice.

"Um." God, what could she say. She wanted to say Yes, but her head told her to say No.

He stopped their walking and kissed the back of her hand.

"Lauren, it's okay. I would like to go away with you and show you the countryside, but perhaps it is too soon. I don't want to make you uncomfortable." His eyebrows pinched together.

She nodded. "Andre, can we play it by ear? Let's see how the day goes tomorrow, but I'd love to go to the wine country with you."

He smiled and accepted her compromise. "Excellent idea."

***

Saturday morning, Andre dropped his overnight bag in the back of his car and drove to

Lauren's hotel. He knew he was already wound a little tight not having Lauren with him in his bed all night.

They had shared an excellent meal, but he didn't push her for anything more. She asked him to walk her back to her hotel, so he did, happily. He knew she felt more comfortable going back alone last night, but *merde!* He wanted to feel her soft, warm body against his all night.

Thoughts, like the ones he had of Lauren, never felt this strong before, even through all his years with Nicolette. He appreciated Lauren's desire not to rush this relationship any more than they had already. Hell, he normally would agree, but there was something about her that stirred him deep inside.

He had to think positively about their trip to *Bourgogne*. He wanted fall asleep with her by his side and wake with her in his arms. He wanted to walk with her and show her the beautiful country. In the evening, they could do many wonderful, intimate things. For now, he would need to keep his thoughts in check.

Breaking his stream of thought, his cell phone rang. He recognized the number—Madam Bonnet, his neighbor of three years.

"Bonjour, Madam Bonnet."

"Andre. How are you? Are you home? I stopped by, but there was no answer."

"No, *madam*. I left a few minutes ago."

"I called to tell you I will be moving out a week early," she said.

"Oh, yes?"

"And I have something for you. Do you think you could stop by sometime today?"

"Yes. This morning would be best. Alright?"

"Parfait." He hung up the phone thinking about his dear old neighbor.

He arrived at Lauren's hotel to find her holding a carry-on bag. His heart jumped. He returned her smile and leaned down to kiss her.

"Good morning."

"Good morning, Andre."

"Ready to see some of the French countryside?"

"Oui."

"We have a short stop to make before driving to the country. Okay?"

"Certainly. Can you tell me where we're going?

He glanced her way briefly. "Yes. I have a neighbor, an elderly woman, whom I've known for years. She is moving in with her son's family. But it wasn't supposed to happen until next weekend."

"Oh."

"She called and has something to give me. She wants to see me today."

"I see." Lauren's lips curved slightly. "She has something for you, that's nice. Are you two very close?"

"In a manner, we are. Over the years she's come to rely on me when her family wasn't around. I would do things for her, help her out."

Thinking about Madam Bonnet moving out brought back reminiscences of happy times he shared with her: her stories, her dry wit, and her heartache over losing her husband. He was deep in thought as he drove back to her apartment building not realizing Lauren had spoken.

"Andre?"

"Yes. I'm sorry. What did you say?"

"What were you thinking about?"

"Madam Bonnet." Absently, he reached over and took a hold of Lauren's hand. "She's a good woman. I am sometimes concerned about her, so I'm glad she will be with her family where they can take care of her." He nodded as he spoke.

They pulled in front of the building and parked. As they climbed the stairs, Lauren saw the door of the apartment next to Andre's open. He knocked on the door frame. "Madam Bonnet?" he called.

"Andre." A little old lady in a green and white dress walked into the living room carrying a stack of newspapers.

He strode inside and leaned down to kiss both her cheeks.

Lauren stood at the doorway watching. She noted how her Frenchman towered gently over Madam Bonnet. And she didn't seem the least bit intimidated.

They spoke in French so fast, Lauren couldn't catch much of the conversation.

Then, Andre turned to her and introduced her to the woman.

"Nice to meet you, dear," Madam Bonnet said with a sparkling smile on her face.

"Hello, nice to meet you."

From the stairwell, Lauren heard several footsteps and voices approaching. A gentleman and two teenage girls approached the apartment.

Andre seemed to recognize the man as Madam Bonnet's son. And the teenagers were her grandchildren. The man greeted and shook hands with Andre as the girls stood stock-still, eyes fixed on Andre, mouths gaping.

Lauren had to smile to herself when the spirited girls took off around the corner, giggling as they went out of sight. She knew that the giggling was about a tall, dark and handsome man who stood in their grandmother's living room.

She noticed what little attention Andre paid to the hormonal girls. Instead, his attention stayed constant on Madam Bonnet.

The lady leaned down to retrieve a wrapped box and handed it to him.

"Open it," she commanded.

He untied the ribbon and ripped the paper off the box. He then opened the box and pulled out a French coffee press. It appeared to be old.

"Ah," Andre exclaimed. "Look at this. This is wonderful. Thank you, madam." His face lit with joy over the gift.

The woman clapped her hands closed in front of her chest and smiled brightly at him.

They chatted more before he leaned down and kissed her cheeks. The woman placed her hand on Andre's cheek. Lauren noticed the evidence of arthritis in her fingers. Then, the woman murmured something about being a good boy. Lauren dropped her head to hide the smile on her face.

"Best of luck to you, Madam Bonnet. Thank you again and take care of yourself," he told her.

"You too, Andre."

Andre strode to the door, and took Lauren's hand without saying a word.

"Goodbye," she called to the woman.

As they went to his car, Andre seemed unusually quiet.

"You worry about her?"

He glanced down at her. "Yes, I supposed I do."

"And you're going to miss her?"

He opened her car door and she ducked inside. He strolled to the back and set his gift gently inside, then opened his car door and got in. For a moment he was silent before he started. "Yes, I'm going to miss her. She is a good woman. As much as I took care of her, she took care of me. I've never met a woman quite like Madam Bonnet."

He started the car. "But she loves her family and they love her, so I know she will be in good hands."

Lauren sat for a moment expecting Andre to say something more. Her gut told her Andre's affections for Madam Bonnet ran deep. Lauren sat quietly. She was uncertain if she pry or leave Andre to his thoughts.

"She gave you a coffee press. It seemed old."

The corner of his mouth rose in a grin. "It is. She has a similar coffee press and she would make us coffee with it occasionally when I visited. She knew how much I enjoyed it."

"That was sweet of her," Lauren murmured.

As they drove, Andre thought more about his neighbor. Despite the fact that he traveled so much, or perhaps because he traveled so much, Madam Bonnet and he had become friends. She was a constant in his life for the past three years. He would eventually adjust to not having her nearby, but he would miss seeing her, miss their chats over coffee.

He decided to push those thoughts aside for a time so he could focus on the trip that lay ahead. His getaway with Lauren.

During the drive, he and Lauren chatted about many things. He loved how she looked after her brother and cared about the spa where she worked, even if the owner was harsh. She asked about his work and travels. She was curious about his family, and her face seemed to light up when he spoke about his parents. She seemed very fascinated by his parents. He hoped one day he could introduce her to them, although that was probably unrealistic.

They arrived at their first winery, not terribly large, but they produced an excellent wine. They passed lush green grape vines as they drove toward the stone building.

He guided Lauren around, hand in hand, and showed her the vineyard and the cellar, filled floor-to-ceiling with oak wine barrels.

They proceeded toward stone steps, about to ascend to the tasting room when Lauren asked, "Have you been here before?"

His stomach cramped. As he opened his mouth to answer, a *petit*, graying gentleman hustled their way.

"Forgive me. Forgive me," he spoke in French. "I was delayed. Welcome to my vineyard." He enthusiastically shook his and Lauren's hands.

"Thank you very much. You have a wonderful vineyard."

The gentleman smiled as he held Lauren's hand and spoke directly to her, "Welcome. Would you like to sample some wine, lovely lady?" Oh, this man was a charmer. He could tell by how Lauren's beautiful face lit up.

"Yes, please," she replied, returning his smile.

The wine was indeed highly rated, just as Andre had remembered it. He purchased several bottles, and they waved goodbye to the owner as they made their way to Andre's car.

They visited three more wineries, and before going further, he needed to know what her decision would be.

"*Chérie*, shall we go to the chateau, check-in, and find a place for dinner? Or shall we find a place for dinner now, and then drive back to Paris?"

He watched her nibble her upper lip, and she lifted her head to face him. He thought he would see worry. Instead, her eyes sparkled.

"I think we should go check in and then find some dinner." She gave him a small smile, barely showing her white teeth.

He reached for her hand and kissed her knuckles. "*Bonne*."

Andre pulled the car into the stone driveway of the little stone chateau and parked in an available spot.

Lauren unhurriedly climbed out of the car with her eyes wide.

"Wow," she said. "This is like a castle, Andre."

He smiled at her and nodded. "*Oui*. I suppose it is. Although it doesn't have as many rooms as some of the other chateaus we could have gone to."

She raised her eyebrows.

A beautiful fountain graced the front gardens, and the large iron door was braced open so they could walk right in. They quickly checked in and were given an overview of the grounds with a map.

The room held a few original sixteenth-century touches with some modern enhancements as well. Lauren gasped when she entered the room. "This is lovely."

A large, high canopy bed was draped in lightweight muslin fabric, and at the other end of the room sat a fireplace. He had to admit, it had a romantic feel. He would create a weekend for them to remember.

"Let's go walk the grounds and look for a restaurant for dinner," he said.

"Sure. Give me a minute," she scurried to the en-suite bathroom.

CHAPTER EIGHT

LAUREN TOOK SEVERAL deep breaths when she was alone in the bathroom. She couldn't believe she was going to spend the night with Andre—a man she met just days ago. As much as she questioned her judgment, the thrill and anticipation of spending a romantic weekend with her gorgeous Frenchman made her nipples peak, and her toes curl. He was abundantly charming and gracious, and she knew if she didn't accept his invitation to spend the weekend in the wine country with him, she would regret it.

Walking the town, they settled on a quaint old-looking restaurant, known for excellent traditional French food. They dined at leisure and finished a bottle of red wine. Andre ordered a bakery-fresh, decadent chocolate cake for dessert for them to share.

After dinner, they strolled on the sidewalks and chatted about Paris, New York, and things they both liked about their hometowns. They dashed into a few shops. Andre bought what looked like essential oil in little boutique and pastries in a bakery. As the night fell, a coolness settled into the town.

"*Chérie*, you do not have a coat. Let us go back to the hotel so you are not cold."

She gave a slight smile and nodded.

He wrapped an arm around her as they made their way back to their room.

"How about I make a fire?" he said with eyebrows raised.

"Sure, that sounds nice."

"Come here, *chérie*," he called her as the fire began to spread over the wood. He held out a hand for her and guided her in front of him to face the fire. "This will warm you."

The heat from the fire enveloped quickly, but as Andre stroked her upper arms, she forgot about the fire. She closed her eyes as he moved his hands to her shoulders and neck, massaging with a firm but gentle touch. He brushed her hair aside and placed little kisses on her neck as his hands continued down her back. The feeling was calm and exciting at the same time.

"*Chérie?*"

"Hmm."

"Perhaps you would like to lie on the bed and I can give you a proper massage?"

Her heart gave a little jump. How could she turn it down when Andre's hands felt positively magical? She nodded, and he clasped her hand to lead her to the side of the bed.

"Lay like this," he directed as he motioned his hand crosswise on the bed.

"Okay." She slipped off her shoes and climbed onto the bed.

"Uh-uh." His voice stopped her mid-way to the center of the bed.

"Sweater off. I have oil."

She gleaned the mischievous smile that spread across his lips.

She smiled to herself. "Okay." From her knees, she pulled off her sweater and tossed it on a chair, and lay face-down on the cushioned bed.

She heard the rustle of the paper bag and Andre unscrew the cap. The bed dipped as he settled in next to her. She felt his warm hands on her lower back. Oh, so divine. He stroked, glided, massaged and pressed. His fingers were soothing on her back muscles.

She expected him to unclasp her bra, but instead he worked around it. After several minutes, he asked, "May I pull off your slacks to massage your legs?"

Her stomach did a summersault. She lifted her head to meet his gentle eyes.

"Okay." She reached under to undo the button and zipper, and he slid the pants down her legs, leaving her panties in place.

She felt Andre's hands, loaded with more oil, caress her legs and feet. He kneaded her muscles and worked his way to her ass. He massaged each cheek by pushing her lacy panties to the center.

Lauren straddled a fine line between relaxation and exhilaration. Andre's constant rhythmic motions over her body started to build the ache between her thighs. She let out a low moan. She had definitely never had a massage like this.

"It feels so good."

"I'm glad you like it."

He gingerly spread her legs wider to stroke and caress her thighs and butt. He lowered her panties an inch to work on her lower back.

He hardly touched any sensitive areas, and yet Lauren found herself panting. His hands slid up her back to undo her bra and push it open. Slowly, he stroked and kneaded her entire back and shoulders, and he pushed her hair aside to massage her neck.

She felt his warm lips on her neck. Without a word, he continued massaging her body while he kissed and licked her neck. She moaned long and arched off the bed slightly letting her bra fall.

Andre swept his hands to her front and massaged her breasts as he had done to her back. Her body shuddered.

"Oh God, Andre," she breathed. She felt the wetness in her panties, and the ache was overpowering.

"*Chérie*, you feel so good. Let me make you feel better."

She tilted her head to look over her shoulder at his rich chocolate heated eyes. She wanted more. Needed more. She needed a release.

"Yes," she breathed.

He leaned down to kiss her lips, gliding his tongue over hers, moving deeply. He pulled back, "Slide off the bed," he commanded.

On her hands and knees, she crawled off the bed and tossed her bra. Andre pulled off his shirt and pants and brought her flush against his chest. His hard cock pressed against her low back. He kneaded her breasts more while kissing and sucking her neck. He slid his hands down to her stomach and slipped his fingers under her panties to slide them down to the floor.

"Step out, *cherie*, and lay your belly on the bed."

She turned to the bed and laid on it while she kept her feet on the floor. She heard Andre strip out of his underpants and sheath his erection. Next, she felt his big, warm hands slide up her thighs and caress her ass.

He leaned over her and whispered in her ear, "Spread your legs wider for me, *ma chérie*."

She did as he bid, spreading her legs as wide as she could while still touching the floor.

He fondled her more and made his way to her sex. He groaned as his fingers grazed her lips. "So wet," he breathed.

His finger twirled over her clit, and she moaned when he slipped his finger inside. He continued his subtle movements for a brief moment before he removed his finger, and she felt his cock at her entrance. How she needed that.

His hands firmly pressed against her thighs as he slid into her wetness. They both moaned like they were feeling the intimate sensation for the first time. He began to slowly pump into her while his hands continued their massage. He kneaded and massaged her back, while making love to her. His every move put her nerves on fire. She moaned unabashedly.

"Oh God, Andre."

He leaned over and whispered in her ear. "Your breasts, *cherie*. Let me massage them."

She pushed up on her elbows, and he cupped his warms hands over his swollen breasts. He toyed with her nipples, and electricity shot down to her sex.

"Ah," she cried out.

He had her from so many angles. He kissed and licked her neck, massaged her breasts, all the while pumping methodically into her dripping sex. His every move brought her climax closer to the surface. She trembled, desperate for release.

"Andre," she panted as her head fall forward.

He didn't stop, nor did he go faster. God, how long she could she go on like this? It was agonizing.

With the rhythm of Andre's controlled thrusts, she felt the slow climb of her climax.

"Unh," she moaned as he hit a delicious spot deep inside her. Her muscles began to contract around him. It had to be the slowest building climax she had ever had. It was otherworldly. Finally, she felt the fireworks explode in her sex and spread through her body in a deliciously long, erotic climax that nearly made her faint. She screamed into the mattress, and Andre picked up speed to finally give in to his own release.

He collapsed over her and panted against her shoulder.

"*Chérie*, how do you feel?" he asked as he pulled out and lay beside her.

"Andre, that was incredible," she breathed. "I have never experienced an orgasm like that before. It was unbelievable."

A small, proud smile graced his face. "I'm so glad you liked it. Seeing the lotion shop in town, gave me the idea. And I love to have my hands on you," his voice dipped.

She loved the way he spoke to her. The words he said. No other man had touched her, reached her core, in that way before. She smiled and kissed his soft lips.

CHAPTER NINE

MR. BERNARD ARRANGED for a hall to host the event. The place was a large, old stone building with high vaulted ceilings. A lovely blown up photograph of Aunt Rosie rested on an easel next to the podium. As Lauren sat in an quiet, empty room, she reviewed her aunt's eulogy before the guests arrived. How does one give a eulogy for someone basically unknown to them? She rubbed at her temples.

Lauren watched as her aunt's friends poured into the hall. Some stopped to sign the memorial guest book, while others browsed the photo albums beautifully displayed by Mr. Bernard.

Lauren wandered around, introduced herself and thanked as many people as she could. She noted the variety of outfits and styles of the attendees—some in suits who looked like business people, some in colorful garb yet still tasteful. One woman wore a kimono. One couple dressed in attire she thought might be African. One gentleman wore a Scottish kilt, and Lauren saw the most beautiful Persian-inspired dress.

Slowly the guests took their seats and filled almost all the available space.

After everyone settled, the hall director announced Lauren. She ambled to the podium, holding her speech on an over-sized index card.

"*Bonjour*. Good afternoon. Please forgive my English, as my French is terribly rusty," she smiled at her audience who chuckled at her joke. "Rosie was my aunt on my mother's side. She was my mother's only sibling. I must confess, I knew little of my aunt because she moved to Paris when I was young. What I do remember was how vibrant and full of life she was.

"My mother and Rosie were very close, although they didn't see each other as often as they wanted. I know, at least, they are together again now in heaven, and that makes me smile." The words were hard to say, especially with the lump in her throat, but Lauren pressed on.

She had a tight grip on the podium; she forced her fingers to unclasp.

"I knew she loved people, and it's evident from the many photos she had, that she loved you all very much."

A woman's sob echoed in the hall.

"I am grateful that you are all here. That you were all a part of my aunt's life. *You* were her family. She is probably looking down smiling, so let's celebrate her life and how she touched each and every one of us. Thank you."

Lauren blinked back the tears and stepped away from the podium. She carefully made her way to her front-row seat, and quickly blotted beneath her eyes with a tissue.

The director approached the mic and announced the first guest speaker.

Lauren sat and listened to story upon story, guest after guest, recounting tales of her aunt. Stories about her generosity, her spunk, her zest for life. Most everyone cried while they spoke and, without exception, everyone smiled or laughed at least once during each talk.

The more she listened, the more her heart swelled. A few times someone said something about Rosie that reminded Lauren of her mom. The similarity was uncanny. After everyone finished, they moved to an adjacent room for refreshments.

Lauren entered the room with the masses. *Wow!* Refreshments might be an understatement. Laid out on covered tables were dish after dish of sumptuous cuisine. Hot covered food, cold food, and a roast beef carving station. Lauren's eyes rounded.

She saw a drink station, many tables covered with white cloths, while music played low in the background. She made her way to the line, stopping several times to receive condolences from attendees. She mentally shook her head. She should be giving *them* her condolences.

She took a seat at a table and within moments, Mr. Bernard approached and stood beside her.

"*Bonsoir, mademoiselle.*"

"Hello, Mr. Bernard," she turned to look up at him, happy to see him. "How are you?"

"I'm fine. May I join you?"

"Certainly," she motioned toward the empty chair beside her.

"I'll get a glass of wine. Would you like one?"

"Yes, please. White."

He returned and settled in the chair, handing her a glass of wine. He took a sip, and he leaned his forearms on the table and furrowed his brow in deep thought. After a moment, he began.

"Your aunt was an incredible woman, Lauren," he spoke in a low tone, looking down at the table. "She was so full of life. She talked about you and your brother sometimes to me. She loved you both." His head tilted to look her way. "She told me about your mother and how much she missed her." He inhaled deeply. Lauren got the impression Mr. Bernard struggled to get his words out. He struggled to keep his emotion in check as well. "Now it is she who will be missed too."

Lauren glanced his way, and although he looked down, Lauren saw the glassiness in his eyes. He sipped his wine again and sat straighter.

Glancing around, he said, "Everyone seems to be enjoying themselves, no?"

"Mr. Bernard, everything is wonderful." She covered his hand with hers. "Thank you for all of your help pulling this together. You did a wonderful job."

His lips curled in a shy smile. "You are quite welcome. I think Rosie would have been pleased."

The evening wound down, and Lauren felt drained. She was used to physically draining days at the spa, but the emotional events she'd confronted lately were far more draining than she expected.

The driver took her back to her hotel. She checked her phone for the hundredth time that day. No texts or emails from Andre. He had told her cell service would be spotty. After merely a week, she shouldn't be so anxious to hear from him. It scared her how quickly she had grown attached to him.

Lauren woke her laptop and opened her email. Cole's email caught her eye immediately. She read about a surprise visit by Regina to the spa. *Oh, no.* As she continued, Cole explained how he'd handled everything and by the time she'd left, Regina was calm again. Lauren exhaled.

"Thank God," she said to no one.

She stood and got ready for bed. The bags under her eyes told her not to delay. She placed her phone on the bedside table and climbed in between the sheets.

***

Andre arrived in Nuuk, Greenland to a primarily low-traffic airport. He read his name on a sign held by a driver in a black suit and cap immediately after arriving in baggage claim.

As he approached, the man smiled and spoke. "*Bonjour. Monsieur* Beauchamp?"

"*Oui*," Andre replied.

"*Parlez-vous Anglais*?

"Yes."

"Terrific. If I can help you with your luggage, the rest of your party is already outside at the van."

Andre picked up his bags, "No, that's okay. I've got it." Because of the extensive and expensive photography equipment, Andre preferred to handle his baggage.

"Very well," the man motioned toward the door and outside Andre found two gentlemen and one woman waiting, chatting in English.

A graying man wearing a cap and glasses saw Andre approach.

"Andre?"

"Yes. Mr. Logan?"

Mr. Logan was the climatologist leading the expedition for the week on a few of Greenland's glaciers. He made the introductions. Andre shook hands and was pleasantly surprised to be greeted by smiling faces and a warm reception.

Andre never knew what to expect when taking trips with strangers, like this. He recalled one trip that included a husband-wife who constantly fought. It made for a rather uncomfortable job. And last year, his trip to Germany was led by a true German—brash, loud and able to drink anyone under the table.

As the van rode through town, Andre snapped several pictures of Nuuk. He was fascinated by the abundance of colorful houses: green, red, blue. He hadn't seen anything quite like it before. As they went, he noted lush green areas while snow lingered in others.

Glancing at his phone, he saw he had decent reception. He shot a short text to Lauren.

Funny, he thought. He was now closer to New York than Paris. During his five-hour flight, Andre did little other than think of Lauren. He wondered how the memorial service went today for her. He wished he could have been there for her.

In the short time he had known her he'd come to see she had a heart of gold. She could stand her ground when necessary and use her savvy business mind. Conversely, she could let her guard down and let the emotion out at other times. Perhaps that was why he so quickly grew attracted to her. She had a smart, quick mind mixed with an abundance of passion. She was honest with him, and he appreciated her willingness to try new things. He couldn't wait to get back to Paris and to her. He wanted to show her more new things. Ah, *oui.* Many more new things.

Pulling him from his thoughts, Mr. Logan proceeded to tell the group a little about the expedition and campsite. *Mon Dieu, it was going to be a long week.*

They would trek to a few different locations for pictures, measurements, and various scientific readings. Andre knew his work these next few days was important, but all he wanted was to get back to Lauren. To feel her arms wrapped around him. To feel her hair against his face. To feel her breasts pressed against his chest. His cock twitched at the mere thought of her.

"So, Andre, do you live in Paris?" said the woman next to him in the back seat. Isabella was her name.

"Yes. And where do you live?"

"Copenhagen, Denmark," she smiled brightly at him. Her blue eyes twinkled when she spoke.

"Ah, I understand Copenhagen to be a very environmentally friendly city, yes?"

"You are correct. I studied climatology there. Learned from some of the best. And I was present at the UN's Climate Change Conference in 2009 which was very interesting."

"So have you been to Greenland before?" he asked, watching her smooth her blond hair off her face.

"Yes. Quite a few times in fact. Greenland is experiencing some significant impact on its environment related to the melting of Arctic ice."

"Oh, really?"

As they continued to talk, he noticed her body language. She leaned toward him, smiled big at little things, touched his arm—she was interested in him. He knew the signs because he'd seen them many times before. He was flattered since she was a beautiful woman, but he could truly say he had no interest in her. She continued to talk, and his thoughts would wander to Lauren.

Without notice, or perhaps because Andre hadn't paid attention, the van pulled into a restaurant outside of Nuuk.

"We will eat here, and then drive for a few hours to our first campsite," Mr. Logan announced from the front seat.

Andre exited with the crew and glanced at his phone. He did a quick calculation. Five-hour flight plus four hours behind . . . Lauren would most likely be asleep by now. And he noticed he had low reception. *Merde!*

They proceeded up the walkway of the large restaurant. Andre hustled to hold the door, allowing everyone to enter before him. He strategically sat last, which placed him next to Mr. Logan and the driver. Excellent. He didn't want to encourage Isabella.

Before meeting Lauren, there was a possibility he would have shared a bed with Isabella. Her curvy body and beautiful smile were the kind of attributes Andre liked. But now since Lauren, no other woman would do. He could wait until Friday.

He ordered a healthy-sized entrée, knowing this would be the last fresh, hot meal for a few days. As they ate, he listened in on the conversation with Mr. Logan and a Swedish scientist when his phone buzzed in his pocket. His heart leaped. *Lauren.*

Lauren had been asleep for an hour when she heard her phone ding with a text. She rose with a start. She reached for her phone and confirmed it was Andre.

Landed in Greenland. I pray your day went well. Miss you terribly. Andre

She immediately replied.

Hi! I'm glad ur safe. Day went better than expected. Stay warm. XX

She sat on the edge of her bed, staring down at her phone. She didn't want to miss him, but she kidded herself to think she didn't miss him already. How was she going to get through this week? *Shit!* She felt like a complete wimp. Since when had Lauren Knight become so dependent on a man before? Seriously.

Slightly disgusted with herself, she flipped the phone on the nightstand and rolled away from the table. She willed herself to stop thinking about him and go back to sleep. She might have succeeded except the phone chimed again. *Andre.*

She scolded herself for the swiftness in which she jumped to the phone.

I'm glad to hear you had a good day. We are eating dinner, then we drive to the first campsite. You should be asleep, chérie. I'll text back when I can. XX

She smiled. He always seemed to look out for her.

She refrained from responding. Instead, she set the phone down and lay back down. She thought wandered to their weekend together. How was it that she trusted a man so soon in their relationship that she would go away with him? It's the sex, she told herself. He made her hot with his touches and wet with his kisses alone. She sighed. She lulled herself to sleep with thoughts of Andre floating in her head.

CHAPTER TEN

ANDRE AWOKE and stared up at his yellow tent. The guy next to him snored lightly. Overall he had a decent sleep—not too cold. Of course, it was nothing like how he slept with Lauren beside him. Her warm body curved into his. Her bare skin flush against his. He groaned inwardly. Don't get excited when you can't do anything about it, he scolded himself.

He gingerly rose and slipped on his jeans and a sweatshirt, careful not to disturb his bunkmate. It wasn't until he slipped on his boots that the smell of coffee rose to his nostrils. *Magnifique.*

He popped out of his tent. In the light, he could appreciate his surroundings better. Their campsite was set up along a riverbed. Across the river in the distance was the point of interest—a large glacier settled into a mountain range. Andre knew he would work first, then they would move closer to the glacier for the climatologists to take their measurements.

"Morning," the driver called to him while working on the breakfast over the campfire.

"Morning," Andre called back.

He walked to a wooded area to take care of business and returned to a bowl of hot water and towels.

"That's for you," the man motioned to the setup. "Can I get you some coffee?"

"Yes, please."

Andre quickly returned to his tent, stripped and gave himself a thorough wipe down and redressed. Coffee awaited his return on the picnic table. He couldn't resist a swig before he took his toothbrush and toothpaste with a water bottle to the side of the river.

When he returned, most everyone was awake and bustling about.

"Morning, Andre. How much time do you need this morning?" Mr. Logan called to him.

"Morning." Andre had already assessed the light and knew, on this clear day, it wouldn't take long to get the shots he needed. "About forty-five minutes to an hour."

"Excellent. Breccan will serve you first, and we'll take down camp while you work."

"Great. Thank you."

After breakfast, Andre took his gear to a clearing along the riverbed that felt approximately where he'd been last year. He retrieved his GPS for exact latitude and longitude coordinates. *Parfait.*

He viewed the glacier through the lens, worked the dials and snapped a few shots. Adjusting the zoom, he snapped several more. Next to the low gurgle of water flowing down the river, the shutter of his camera was the only sound in this pristine wilderness. What an amazing country.

He moved several meters north, verified his coordinates and shot several more photos. He paused long enough to retrieve several smaller photos from last year's expedition from his bag. He studied the photos of the glacier. The evidence was there before him. The glacier had shrunk. Andre loaded his equipment and shook his head. What a shame, he thought.

***

Tuesday, Lauren arrived at her aunt's house a few hours earlier than she expected the real estate agent to arrive. She did a walk-through making sure everything was in place.

The walls and trim were painted in most of the rooms to a pleasant neutral color. Furniture had been situated to make rooms look as spacious as possible. Personal items and tchotchkes were mostly packed away, opening the space up more. Countertops and floors gleamed. The landscape looked lush and well-manicured in the front and back yards.

Lauren smiled as she adjusted a fruit bowl on the kitchen island. The house was ready for a new owner.

Corinne walked into the house, her eyes aglow.

"Lauren, everything looks wonderful," she exclaimed. "The view from the street is perfect, and I love what I'm seeing in here." She wandered around slowly, entering each room, scanning every surface. She nodded and smiled. "The color for the walls is perfect. Not too light, not too dark."

She returned from perusing the second floor and met Lauren in the kitchen.

"*Bonne.* Let's take some pictures for the agency listing."

Corinne seemed to be pleased with the progress made in the last week. Lauren walked her to the door. Corinne's smile broadened. "I'll keep you posted. Now is just time to wait." She leaned in, placed a kiss on each of Lauren's cheeks, and said, "I'll be in touch."

"Thank you." She watched Corinne make her way to her car.

Lauren smoothed her lips together and exhaled. *What to do now.*

***

The last full day and night in Greenland, and Andre would fly home. He could do this. He thought of Lauren on his downtime. Hell, he thought of her all the time. Images of her smile and the twinkle in her eye occupied his thoughts. He could still recall her lush, soft hair, and the unique smell at her throat and between her breasts. He knew for certain he had at least two wet dreams of her. He sighed inside.

Scoping out the area of their last locale, Andre took in the view. Ice everywhere. They literally camped on a glacier. That day the climatologists would drill down and retrieve a sleeve of ice to take back to a lab and examine. The information gained on this expedition would be published and presented to the French government and the U.N. This is surreal, he thought.

Isabella came to his side interrupting his thoughts.

"Andre, we should take a selfie." She lifted her cell phone to show him.

He nearly rolled his eyes. He understood pop culture and the proliferation of social media, but as a professional photographer, he didn't always appreciate it.

Isabella snaked an arm under Andre's and across his low back. With her other hand, she held her phone out, and a shutter sounded. He bit back a chuckle.

"Here," she stuck her phone in his hand. "Your arm is longer. You take the picture, Andre." And as he held an arm outward, she wrapped her other arm around his waist and pulled herself snug against his body. She was too close, her sickie-sweet perfume flew into his nostrils and nearly made him gag.

He pasted on a fake smile and pressed the button. Are we done? he thought.

"Great. Now let's get one over here."

Oh, no you don't.

"Sure, but Isabella, I'm being a hog. Breccan," he called a few meters away, "come here and take a picture with Isabella."

Isabella's face fell. And Andre didn't care. Breccan, on the other hand, never looked happier.

"Sure," he called as he jogged over to them and dropped on arm over Isabella's shoulder. The smile on her face dimmed compared to moments earlier. As Andre snapped, he debated calling over the other men to join in.

After two shots, Isabella nearly leaped to retrieve her phone.

"Thanks, Andre. I better put it away now, so I don't run out of battery."

He watched her walk back to her tent, and he turned to hide the full smile on his face.

***

Andre's plane landed a few minutes ahead of schedule, and he couldn't be happier. He was anxious to see Lauren. He missed her. Cell service from his location in Greenland was nonexistent. The team leader had a satellite phone, but he hesitated asking to use it to call his girlfriend.

He powered on his phone as the plane taxied to the terminal.

"Hello?"

His eyes closed blocking out everything but her voice. She sounded so sweet. He missed hearing her voice.

"Hello, *chérie*. Are you at your hotel?"

"Andre! You've landed? Yes, I'm at the hotel. Come over."

"I'll be right there."

He arrived at Lauren's hotel and knocked on her door. He willed his heart to calm. She opened the door wide, and looked him up and down.

"What took you so long?" she asked with a sexy little smirk across her lips.

She wore a red silk nightgown that went just past her ass. Her peaked nipples on her full bosom made his mouth water. And he would bet his last euro that she wasn't wearing any panties.

"Come here." He grabbed her by her waist, pushed her up against the door, and crashed down onto her pretty mouth with his. He ravaged her. He reached down, lifted one of her legs to his hip, and she pressed into him. She moaned into his mouth as she wrapped her arms around his neck. He slid his hands over her ass—no panties—and pulled her closer into his jeans-clad erection. They both groaned.

He slipped a finger over her sex and found it slippery wet. He thrust a subtle little rub, and she whimpered. Then his hands went north and cupped her curvaceous breasts. He dragged his thumbs over her plump nipples.

"I missed you," he murmured against her lips.

He backed away and without hesitation grabbed the red gown, pulled it over her head and threw it. With both hands cupped on her breasts, he leaned down and took a nipple in his mouth.

"Andre," she moaned and reached between them to get her hands on his belt. She made fast work of the buckle, button, and zipper. Before she pushed his pants down, she reached into his back pockets and found a condom. Damn, smart lady!

His cock flexed. He felt desperate to get inside her.

She pushed his jeans and briefs past his hips, and wrapped her hands around his urgent erection. He flexed his hips, stretching in her hands. She ripped open the wrapper with her teeth and unrolled the condom over his cock.

"Make it good, big boy," she cajoled.

"Oh yeah," he replied in a deep, throaty voice.

With no more ceremony, he drove deep into her pushing her farther up the door. He grabbed her ass cheeks, lifted and held her.

She cried out.

He froze. "*Chérie*! I'm sorry. Did I hurt you?"

"No. Don't stop." She swung her other leg around and linked her ankles behind him. He started his grind with a singular focus. He went at it with such force; he ravished her. She let go of him and spread her arms over her head, flat against the door. She arched into him to get more friction from the movement.

"Oh," she called out. "Oh," again, breathing heavily.

He tipped his head down to her raised bouncing nipples, took one in his mouth, flicked it with his tongue and sucked hard. He sucked the other nipple and bit lightly. She cried out. Seeing her excited only made him hotter; he knew he had only moments left before he'd explode.

"Ah," she called out.

And after an instant, they both came, a fierce tornado coursing through them. She screamed, and he grunted loudly, and he didn't care who heard. Needing to catch his breath, he wrapped his arms around her torso and held her as they sank to the floor to recuperate.

She rolled off him onto the floor, both of them on their backs, looking up. Their breathing slowed. She was the first to break the silence.

"Boy, you've got some fire in you tonight," she grinned, her chest still rising and falling with her breaths.

He turned to look at her and smiled. "I'm just getting warmed up." His eyebrows wiggled.

She chuckled. "Well, how about a drink?" She rose and shrugged on the white hotel robe.

He furrowed his brows. He hadn't expected her to get up. He rose, disposed of the condom in the bathroom, and yanked up his jeans.

She handed him a shot of whiskey. *Whiskey? Did she drink hard liquor?*

"Lauren, how was your week? Everything go okay?" He asked as he sat on the bed.

She took a sip and met his eyes.

"It was real good. I'm finished with my aunt's house. The agent took pictures of the place."

He nodded, expecting her to expand. "Was that all you did this week? Work on the house?"

She tipped her head and planted a sexy little smirk on her lips. "Aside from picking up men at the hotel bar, yes."

His eyes went wide at the unexpected comment. *What?*

She grinned. "I'm just kidding."

Her face heated as she strolled over to stand in front of him, between his legs. She set down her drink on the nightstand, reached for his glass and placed it next to hers.

"Are you quite through?" Keeping his gaze, she untied the robe sash, slipped the garment off her shoulders and let it fall to the floor.

His heart rate picked up as he watched her unveil herself before him. His nostrils flared, and his breath sputtered. "*Merde.*"

Something was off tonight with Lauren. If it wasn't related to the house, what was it? His cock came alive watching her strip for him. He needed to make love to her again, but he would find out what was eating at her before the night ended.

His eyes roamed her naked body, and he stood. She stepped back to give him room. He whipped off his shirt, then he reached down and lifted her over his shoulder. She squealed. He smacked her creamy ass.

"I need a shower."

"Andre," she squealed again. He swatted her behind again.

With one hand, he undid his pants button and zipper as he walked. He trotted into the bath and turned the water on hot. With one hand he pushed his pants off, set her in the shower and stepped in after her.

Water pounded on them and over them. He grabbed her face and kissed her lips, her neck, and descended slowly to her breasts.

She moaned.

He raised his head. "I missed you, *cherie*." He looked directly into her eyes. Searching for something. "Tell me you missed me."

Something flashed over her face so fast he almost missed it. A sly little smile slid over her lips.

"I missed this," she glossed her hand over his cock.

He jumped back in surprise.

"*Merde*," he snapped. He pulled his hands from her face to slam the tile, straddling her head. It would have felt better to punch through that tile wall instead. "No, Lauren. Me. Did you miss me?"

She bit her lips and glanced down. Had she been that obvious? She couldn't get to the heart of her issue, her discomfiture. She had missed Andre. Terribly. But she didn't want to. To make matters worse, they had two weeks left, and he couldn't matter this much to her. Couldn't.

"What? I see that brain working, Lauren. Tell me the truth. What is going on?"

How could she make him understand?

"I," she glanced up into his eyes, "I missed you, Andre. I don't want to miss you. I leave to go back to New York in two weeks," she pleaded. Tears threatened, and she tried to control them.

He brushed a hand against her cheek. His voice low and pensive,

"Don't be sad. We'll cross that bridge when we get to it. Yes?"

She nodded because, what could she do about it now? Send him away. Not likely.

He lifted her chin with his fingertips.

"Kiss me, *cherie*."

She brought her arms to his shoulders and rested her hands on his neck. Lifting herself on her toes, she licked his lower lip and gently bit it. He moaned into her mouth. Her tongue slipped into his delicious mouth and caressed, soothed.

His body, hard against hers, felt hot. His lush erection lay flush on her stomach. He kissed her with pure passion. Her sex filled with liquid heat.

"God, Andre. You feel so good," she breathed against his lips. "Please."

"Anything you want, *cherie*," he whispered back.

Her lips cooled when he pulled back to reach into his pants pocket for a condom. He covered himself and grasped her waist with his warm hands.

"Hold on to me." He lifted her and she wrapped her legs around his narrow waist while clinging to his shoulders.

Releasing one hand, he held himself to slide into her. She bowed off the tile wall and moaned.

"*Ma chérie*," Andre whispered more in French into Lauren's neck as he sucked and nibbled her sensitive skin. She didn't understand his words, but she felt certain it was laced with lust and emotion.

"Ah," she groaned as her swollen sex began to clench around his shaft. "Andre," her voice a little higher. She couldn't hold back any longer as he continued his thrusts. "Andre," she screamed aloud, letting the ripples of pleasure course through her entire body.

He pumped into her several more times when he released. He grunted and crushed his mouth over hers for one last kiss of pure desire.

He brought them to the tub floor, and in a haze she was aware that he plugged the drain and switched off the shower to fill the tub. He spun them around so she lay on top of him. She heard his heartbeat as she rested on his chest, and slowly her level breathing returned.

"Are you feeling okay?"

"Yes. I feel more than okay." Her arm wrapped tighter around his waist.

He brought his arms around her and kissed the top of her head. She felt utterly content.

His words echoed in her mind. Andre was probably right. They would decide what they would do about their relationship, affair, whatever, in a few weeks. She grimaced internally. Lauren had the distinct feeling it would mean a tearful goodbye.

CHAPTER ELEVEN

LAUREN AWOKE to the sun with a smile on her face. Andre spent the night with her, and her body hummed even in the morning. She seemed to glow from the inside out.

Her head rested on his bare chest, and she could easily let the sound of his beating heart lull her back to sleep. But as if he'd known she was awake he said, "Good morning, *chérie*." He kissed the top of her head.

"Morning," she smiled and lifted her head enough to kiss his chest.

"I was thinking of taking you to Versailles today. Do you have any plans?"

"No. I'd love to go," she said gazing into his beautiful face.

"*Bonne*. Can you be ready in an hour or so?"

"Yes."

He smiled, kissed the top of her head, and threw the covers off them to stand.

The elation of waking in Andre's arm popped like a balloon. He must have seen her face fall.

"*Chérie*, if I don't get out of bed now, we'll never get out of here." Flashing his pearly whites and dimple, he leaned down, planted a kiss on her lips and rose. "I promise, I'll make it up to you," his eyes heated as he spoke. She smiled, and he turned to head for the bathroom.

Andre pulled his Smart car up to the curb in front of her hotel at precisely nine. She jogged out looking adorable. Her hair was clipped away from her face. She wore a floating skirt that stopped at the knees with a pale purple cardigan layered over a white button-down and ballet flats.

He stepped out of the car and swung around to greet her.

"You look lovely, *chérie*." He leaned down to kiss her soft lips.

"Thank you, *monsieur*."

As he pulled into traffic, she asked, "Will you drive us the whole way there or will we take the train?"

His brow rose. "I'll drive. Why?"

"Oh, no reason except I thought with the long distance . . ."

"Are you making fun of my car again?"

She clamped her lips closed and shook her head. The twinkle in her eye betrayed her; she held back a smile.

"Would you rather take the train?"

She tilted her head to the side and bit the inside of her cheek. "Would we have a private car?" she asked.

"Oh, *chérie*. Do not tempt me." He reached across for her hand, brought it to his lips and kissed her knuckles.

She flashed her beautiful smile at him. He held her hand because it felt good in his.

After a thirty-minute drive, they found a place to park close to Versailles. He grabbed the picnic basket from the trunk and took her hand to walk to the chateau.

"I thought we could walk through the chateau first, and before going to Marie Antoinette's house, we can lunch in the gardens."

"Whatever you say," she looked up at him with a smile.

The line progressed and, in several short moments, they were inside. Her eyes grew large with the grandeur and opulence around them.

As they walked with the crowd, he snapped a few pictures, mostly of his beautiful lover. She asked questions, and he explained the best he could.

"The signing of the Peace Treaty of Versailles in 1919 took place here in the Hall of Mirrors."

She cleared her throat. "Andre, I have to admit. I'm not up on French history."

He understood. He'd run into Americans now and again. Their lessons in history seemed mostly focused on America, and not so much the world.

"The peace treaty contributed to the ending of World War I. The European Allied powers imposed the Treaty on the already defeated Germany. Germany had to concede a lot of land and territory. Also, Germany had to agree to take fault for the entire war and was considered responsible for all material damages."

"Oh, that's interesting," she nodded.

They walked the entire palace with the crowd, and afterward, made their way out back to the gardens.

"Oh, Andre." Lauren's eyes went wide surveying the expanse of land in front of them.

He pointed out the Apollo Fountain, the canal, rectangular pools, sculptures, and statues. They walked far out along the oversized pools, halfway to Marie Antoinette's house, when Andre saw the perfect spot. A grassy area along the pool with a backdrop of an abundance of trees.

"Let's sit and eat our lunch over there," he pointed to the other side of the pool away from the crowds.

"Okay."

He took her hand and led her off the sidewalk around the enormous pool. They spread out a blanket on the grass, and she got comfortable. He pulled the food out of the basket. She helped him set up the cheese and smoked salmon with *pain* while he opened a bottle of wine.

"What a perfect day," she sighed and looked up to the blue sky.

He snapped a profile view of her angelic face when she glanced to the heavens. "It is."

She turned his way at the sound of the shutter and grinned.

"Put that away," she teased.

He set his camera down and poured a glass of wine for her.

"Since being in France, I don't think I've had so much wine in my life," she grinned again.

"Yes? Well, this is a bottle we got last weekend on our trip to *Bourgogne*, and if I recall correctly, you enjoyed it." He sent her a sly smile and a wink.

Oh yes, their trip to Burgundy. She never had so much sex in her life. She knew much had to do with the fact that Andre would be gone the following five days to Greenland. He certainly had a healthy appetite for sex—she smiled to herself—not that she minded.

"What made you decide to become a photographer?" she asked.

"I'm not sure exactly. I would take pictures as a hobby, you could say, and I enjoyed seeing the finished product. I love to travel, and as my photography improved, my two joys in life merged. Or perhaps because I love to travel, I used photography as a means to an end." He gave her a devilish grin, and bit a piece of bread.

They lounged on the blanket and noshed on Andre's packed lunch.

"I feel so Parisian," she quipped.

He reclined back on one elbow, a glass of wine in his other hand. "You look *Parisienne* sitting there, *chérie*."

She popped a grape in his mouth and one in hers. And like a thunderbolt out of nowhere, a thought struck her. How many women has he brought here like this?

Andre had the most incredible way of making her feel special but, was this a gift he had with all women?

She took a good gulp of wine, chasing down the lump in her throat. This affair is temporary, she reminded herself. It didn't matter how many women he had been with before her.

"*Chérie*? What are you thinking about?"

"Oh, nothing really. Thank you for bringing me here." She mirrored his position, balancing her weight on one elbow. "It is beautiful. And peaceful."

He brushed a stray hair from her face and leaned forward to gently kiss her lips.

"You are beautiful," he breathed against her lips.

She smiled. He kissed her again only deeper this time. And longer. She sank into him, feeling the heat radiate from his body. He moved back enough to take the glass from her hand. He placed them both behind him.

He turned to face her again, and with a hand on her waist he pulled her close to his body. He kissed her, sliding his tongue into her mouth deeply, seeking hers. He groaned and laid her down, resting his hot body over hers. She felt his growing erection at the crux of her thigh.

She could get high on his kisses alone. His mouth felt hot and velvety-soft mingling with hers.

She felt his fingers ease apart some buttons on her shirt. Her body stiffened.

She pushed against his shoulders, breaking the kiss.

"Andre, we can't do this here."

"We won't, *chérie*."

She narrowed her eyes.

"I promise. No one can see us over here when they are all the way over there across the water."

She saw the sincerity in his eyes. A thrill of being slightly naughty in public raced through her.

He slipped a few buttons on her blouse and discreetly eased his fingers inside. While he had her distracted with his sensuous, heated kisses, he pushed open her blouse and slid the material from her bra under her breast, one at a time.

The heat raced through her body and peaked her nipples. She felt moisture start to pool and dampen her panties.

"Andre," she moaned, beseeching him to stop.

"They cannot see, *cherie*."

His body completely covered hers from view, and he inched his fingertips to circle over her eager nipples. She arched into his hands and mewled. He played as he kissed her neck, right at a sweet little spot under her ear. She writhed against him.

She held his head with her two hands, grabbing fistfuls of dark, full hair. Lightly she pulsed her hips against him.

"What are you doing to me?" she breathed.

"I was thinking the same thing."

Suddenly to her great surprise, he covered her breasts and buttoned up her blouse. Her heart sank. She didn't mean to imply that they should stop. Reasonably dressed, he pushed off the ground and tossed the containers into the basket. *Oh no.*

"What are you doing?"

He looked down at her and offered his hand. His eyes showed deep and dark. "Come with me."

She licked her lips, took his hand and stood. They gathered their belongings and holding her hand, led her toward the treed area.

"Andre?"

He glanced at her. "I have an idea," was all he said.

Oh my. Yes, her man always had an idea.

She watched her step as they walked farther away from the main gardens. A little deeper into the woods, he stopped, scanned the area and announced, "This is good."

He set down the basket, camera, and blanket, and yanked her up against him.

"This is perfect," he murmured against her lips. Holding her, he backed her two steps against a large tree and his mouth covered hers. Her tongue reached for his, and her arms swung around his neck.

He worked her buttons again, and in a swift move, he pulled her breasts from her bra. His mouth lowered and sought out a nipple. He laved at it with his tongue and gently nipped. She moaned and pulled at his hair.

"Andre," she whispered.

The achiness at her sex now made her needy. She knew having sex outside at a national attraction, no less, was risky. But perhaps that added to the thrill.

She wanted him inside her. She couldn't recall ever needing a man so desperately.

She drew her hands to his pants to release his button and zipper. She reached in and grabbed his cock. She stroked his bulbous tip and shaft. He moaned against breast.

He lowered his body, pulling himself out of her hands. His hands glossed up her legs and his fingertips smoothed over her wet panties.

"I love your body, *chérie.*" He lifted her skirt and added, "Hold this here."

She did as he commanded, and without hesitation, he whipped her panties down and stroked his fingers over her nether lips. His tongue dove into her, and she whimpered, flexing her hips toward his face. His expert moves brought more cream to the surface. She nearly shook with need.

"Andre, please."

He looked up at her. He stood to don a condom and bid her to turn around. She placed her hands on the tree trunk and arched her back for him. He lifted her skirt and smoothed his hands over her ass, sending a shiver up her spine. He placed himself at her entrance and slowly slid inside her. They both moaned aloud.

His hands slid up to cup her breasts while he moved inside her. "I don't want these beautiful breasts to be scratched, *chérie*," he whispered in her ear.

He kissed and sucked her neck while he slowly gained speed. Her legs widened, and she pressed back against his gyrations. Her panting was as loud as his. She felt a tightening inside as his cock stroked her joyous spot.

"Ah," she moaned. "Oh God."

Andre didn't let up.

"I want to feel you, *chérie*."

In no time, she shattered. Her climax released inside her with an explosion of sensation that made her legs weak. Andre held her upright and continued his pumping until she heard his low growl at her neck as he ejaculated.

She let her head fall forward, gasping for air.

"Andre, you are a sex fiend."

He chuckled in her hair. "*Oui*. For you."

She turned in his arms, and he brought his lips crashing over hers. The kiss was long, sensual and passionate. It was one of the first things she grew to love about Andre.

They dressed and snuck out of the treed area as if nothing unusual happened. He held her hand as they strolled to Marie Antoinette's house and gardens. The day went beyond her expectations. She couldn't keep the smile off her face.

Anytime the thought of returning to New York popped in her head, she quickly squashed it down. She wanted nothing to burst her little bubble of happiness.

CHAPTER TWELVE

THE NEXT DAY, Lauren and Andre had plans for lunch.

For reasons she couldn't point a finger on, Lauren woke in a funk. She thought a massage at the hotel's spa would help, but it didn't.

In the back of her mind lingered the question about Andre and his previous girlfriends. How was it such a kind, caring and good-looking man was still on the market? Surely, he'd been married or at least engaged? Maybe there was something wrong with him? Her heart stopped.

They really hadn't known each other that long. *Geez!*

Alright, her imagination was getting the best of her.

It shouldn't matter, she scolded herself. She would return to New York in a few weeks. She had her aunt's estate to handle, and then a spa awaited her. The time she spent with Andre was pure gravy. *Don't make this bigger than it is.*

Andre sensed something was off the minute he met Lauren at her hotel. Her shoulders were tight and he felt an uneasiness rolling off her. He saw tension and worry in her eyes. It didn't feel the same as when she grappled with her aunt's house or her parents' death. So what was it?

They had an exceptional time together the day before at Versailles. She glowed the whole day. He had wanted to be with her last night, make love to her until they fell asleep, but he didn't push his luck.

She smiled at him, but it didn't touch her eyes. Not like all the times before.

They walked the city streets, slowly meandering their way to the restaurant. He broke the silence.

"Lauren, is there something wrong?"

"What would make you ask that?"

Why was she deflecting?

"I get the sense that something is on your mind. Something you might not want to talk about." He stopped, so she did too. "You can talk to me about anything, *chérie*."

She glanced down, then back up to him and nodded.

"I find myself thinking about previous girlfriends you might have had." She shrugged her shoulders. "It shouldn't matter, but you are handsome and kind, and yet still single. I don't understand."

"Let's sit," he said as he pointed toward a bench along an open grassy area. He inhaled. "My last relationship ended six months ago."

"How long were you together?"

"Almost seven years."

She gasped. He felt a jolt of tension in her hand. He knew this was going to sound rough at first, but she needed to hear the truth. He had nothing to hide.

"Her name was Nicolette. We were engaged to be married."

She gasped again and pulled her hand out of his.

"Why did you break up?"

"We decided we didn't have enough in common anymore."

"What? Seven years together and suddenly," her eyes narrowed. "Who broke it off?"

"She did."

Lauren's head shook and the color faded from her cheeks.

"Lauren, it was a situation where we had been together for so long, getting married seemed to be the next logical step. The problem was we didn't share enough similar interests.

"She's a professor at *universite* and teaches economics. She excelled in her career, but it meant more time away from me. Time for us. She spoke at symposiums, wrote and published papers, and taught several hundred students every week for nine months a year.

"I wanted to travel and see the world, and she wanted to stay back. She felt like she was cheating her students, her fellow teachers, whomever, if she didn't stay in Paris and make herself accessible to them.

"After some time, that distance took a toll on our relationship. She broke it off, but I had been thinking the same thing. We could not go on the way we were. If we had gotten married, it certainly would have ended in divorce."

She looked at him with wide eyes. "Did you love her?"

"Yes."

"Do you still love her?"

"No." He frowned and shook his head.

"Have you had girlfriends since Nicolette?"

"Nothing serious."

He watched her face go expressionless, and her spine straightened. *Merde!* She misunderstood.

"Lauren, please know that it was nothing serious, but as for you and me—"

She raised her hand. "No, you don't owe me an explanation." She inhaled. "If you don't mind, I'd like to return to my hotel."

Non!

"Okay. I will walk you."

"No, please don't. I know the way," she stood swiftly, pivoted on a heel. He witnessed her brisk walk back toward her hotel.

It took all his strength to let her go and not to run after her. It killed him.

Oh, God! He had been with a woman for seven years, and they were engaged to be married. The whole thing stung like a sonofabitch. Her chest felt so tight she struggled for a full breath. Why didn't he tell her earlier? Not that that made any sense. She and Andre knew each other less than two weeks. So why the damn reaction?

Andre was a catch, no doubt about it. She liked spending time with him. The thought that he had shared with Nicolette some of the same things he shared with her, turned her stomach. God, she was blind. Of course, he would have been with someone, close to marriage. How could she compete with that history?

She felt the walls of her hotel room closing in on her. She couldn't be there. She grabbed her key and hurried out the front door of the hotel. She paced the streets not totally sure where she was heading.

Her mind raced. She was jealous. She needed to face it.

He is with you now.

But for how long?

She was a pile of contradictions. Why was she having such an adverse reaction to this? Her stomach felt as heavy as lead. She wanted to cry.

By five o'clock, Andre was on his sixth cigarette and his fourth drink. After Lauren had left, he returned to his apartment, parked his car and walked to a dive bar he had frequented several times when he was with Nicolette.

He drank and sometimes smoked then too. Only when it got really bad.

Josh, the bartender, recognized him the moment he walked in. Josh was a good man; he kept the drinks coming, even stopping at his table for a spell.

"Want to talk about it?" he said in French.

"Not really. She's going to need some time, that's all."

"Nicolette?" Josh tipped his head.

"No. I met someone new. She's American. She's lovely. Beautiful and smart and has so much passion."

"Ah. Americans can be fiery," the bartender said with a twinkle in his eye.

"Oui."

Andre checked his phone for the millionth time since watching Lauren leave him. He needed to stick to his words. She just needed time and she would come around. She had to come around. He was falling for her in a serious way. What he felt with Lauren, he never felt with Nicolette. Not even close.

By nine o'clock, he knew he was drunk. He stood, gained his balance after a bit and stumbled home. He managed to get the key in the door and get his shoes off. He collapsed on his sofa and placed his phone on the floor beside. *Lauren.*

He fell asleep with thoughts of her on his mind. His heart ached. Tomorrow. He prayed that she'd call him tomorrow.

***

Lauren was wrong. She wanted to know about Andre's past, he told her about it, and she chastised him for it. What had happened in the past shouldn't matter to them now, she repeated to herself the next morning on her way to Andre's apartment.

She acted like he cheated on her. She had no right to judge, to be upset. Why had she acted like a juvenile? The foolishness of her actions made her cheeks redden.

Not to mention, this relationship was temporary. She would leave in a few weeks for America.

The cab dropped her off at his apartment. She rang the doorbell and held her breath. She hoped with all her might that he would forgive her.

She rang the bell again. God, what if he wasn't home? It was Monday. Did he have a trip? *God, please, no.*

After the third ring, she felt a knot form in her stomach. He wasn't home. She missed her chance. When would he come home? Tears pricked the backs of her eyes.

She turned and looked down at the curb. The taxi was gone. *Dammit!* How many more things could she screw up? She descended the stairs when she heard a door open behind her. Her heart jumped, and she ran back up the steps.

"*Quoi?*" Andre growled as he opened the door, leaning against the doorjamb. He wore the same clothes he had on the day before.

"Andre." She made it before he could close the door.

"Lauren. You're here."

He looked rough, but oh, so beautiful. The stubble on his face made her want to stroke her fingers along his jaw and kiss him all over. She caught the smell of cigarette that wafted off his body. His eyes were glassy. The way he held the door frame, she thought he must have been drinking.

She bit her lips between her teeth. She blamed herself.

"Shall I come back another time?"

"No. God, no. Please come in." He reached his hand out for her but didn't touch her. She took a breath and reached for his hand.

"Andre, have you been drinking?"

"Yes, yesterday. After you left."

He drank because of you. "Were you smoking too?"

"Yes." He glanced down at her hand in his. "Would you please wait a few moments while I shower?"

Her lips and jaw softened, and she nodded.

He paused a moment, maybe to contemplate if she was sincere about staying.

Lauren sank to the sofa. It felt warm. He must have slept on the sofa all night. She sighed. That couldn't have been comfortable.

She did all this. She screwed up their day yesterday, making them both feel miserable. She needed to make it up to him.

She heard the water turn on. Andre would be hopping in the shower at any moment. She glanced back. Hmm, she thought. How much penance did she owe him? She nibbled on her bottom lip. Probably a lot.

She slipped off her shoes and retrieved a hair clip out of her purse. As she made her way back to the bathroom, she shed her clothes. She quietly opened the door to find Andre's head tipped down and water pummeling his muscular, tall, European-tanned body. He scrubbed his hands over his face and through his head. Shampoo bubbles cascaded down his body.

She pushed back the shower curtain, and he whipped around. His eyes wide, he raked over her naked body.

"I came to help you wash your back," she stepped into his shower.

As if he thought he hallucinated, he stood watching her every movement. Not saying a word.

She reached for the bar of soap and a washcloth, and lathered the cloth. "Turn around, please."

His eyes softened, and he presented his back to her. She placed the washcloth on his back, and her other hand on his upper arm for balance. She made small circles all over his broad shoulders and back. Defined and muscular. Next, her hands moved to his arms. One at a time, she stroked the cloth up and down his strong arms. Her hand moved to his firm, curved ass. She might have stayed there a bit longer than necessary. Lastly, she squatted, running her hands up and down his legs. She heard what might have been a groan when she stroked upward.

Fine droplets of water hit her face. She stood.

"Please turn around again."

He spun around to face her. She gleaned Andre's growing erection through her lashes as she lathered her washcloth. She began soaping his chest, slowly. She looked up to find him watching her.

"I'm sorry, Andre. I was wrong."

"Chérie—"

"Shh," she rose up on her toes to place a small kiss on his lips to hush him.

She let her hands wander lower, massaging the cloth over his cock. His eyelids fell half-mast, and he moaned aloud. She cleaned his beautiful member and proceeded down his legs again because she couldn't stop touching him. Seeing him before her, completely naked, he was an Adonis.

She stood again. Fire in his eyes now.

"Rinse please," her voice rasped. Seeing his reaction to her ministrations made her hot, and her sex began to ache.

She reached around to the front of him, her chest to his back. She smoothed her hands over his chest and stomach, and down to his hard cock. She stroked him several times, but Andre couldn't seem to take it anymore.

He spun around and grabbed her face between her hands and crashed his lips onto hers. He thrust his tongue, and she willingly met him, moaning into his mouth. He tasted of mint and hot male.

Remembering her reason for being there, she dropped to her knees. Where she would beg for forgiveness.

With one hand, she wrapped Andre's delicious cock and swiped her tongue over the satiny tip. Lauren hadn't usually been a fan of giving head, but right then, she wanted to please Andre more than anything. She had to have him in her mouth, to taste him, to make him come.

She laved up and down with her tongue, adding a gentle suck. She closed her lips around him completely and took him as far as she could. He let his head fall back and rested his hands on her shoulders. She worked him up and down, moved her hand with her mouth, and sucked on the way out. She persisted, and he growled.

Slowly his hips flexed.

"Fuck." He held her head gently and continued to pump into her mouth.

She sucked harder bringing his orgasm closer to the edge until he exploded wildly into her mouth. He groaned and gasped for air. She swallowed him entirely.

He lifted her and brought her into his chest. "*Mon Dieu.* That mouth."

She smiled into his chest.

He brought her back so he could look in her eyes. She was mesmerized with his pools of chocolate that showed his appreciation and passion and something more. Before she could analyze it further, he reached to switch off the water.

"Come with me," he said in a deep, husky voice as he grabbed her hand and stepped out of the shower. He reached for a bath towel and wrapped it around her. He did the same for himself.

Next, his hand wrapped around hers, and they crossed to the bedroom. He loosened the towel she held and gingerly dried her skin with it. He blotted her cheeks, neck, chest, arms, and back. He stooped down before her and ran the towel over each leg. A shiver ran through her. The shower was merely a prelude. The time and care he took had her panting and achy for more.

He dropped the towel and caressed his hands over her legs making his way to her sex. He smoothed a finger over her slick lips. She inhaled sharply.

"Sit on the bed, *chérie.*"

Oh yes, please.

He laid her down and kissed her feverishly as his fingers stroked her sex. He slipped a finger into her channel, and she bowed off the bed.

"Oh."

"I missed you," he whispered against her neck.

His words squeezed around her heart like a vise. Thank God he took her back.

He continued his pleasurable assault before stopping to reach for a condom inside his bedside table. The towel dropped, and he donned the condom. He positioned himself right at her opening, leaned over her, laced his fingers through hers and pushed inside.

"Oh God," she breathed.

She hooked her legs around him as he pumped into her with controlled movements. She needed more. She was on the edge.

"Andre," she said against his lips.

When he pulled out, she gasped at the sudden emptiness.

"Shh," he told her.

Crouching between her legs, he smoothed his hands over her thighs, spreading her before his mouth came down over her sex. He licked and stroked her lips and clitoris.

"Ah," she cried out.

He worked his tongue over her, never inserting his fingers. God, he was killing her.

He suddenly pulled back and leaned over her, pushed her hands in the mattress and pressed his delicious cock inside her again. She panted as loudly as he did. The sensations he brought out in her, built in her, were like nothing she'd ever experienced before.

He stopped again and leaned down to take her clit in his mouth. Oh God, how much more could she take?

His tongue worked magic against her dripping sex. She rode the next wave higher. She was so damn close to exploding on his tongue.

"Ah," she breathed. "Don't stop."

He stayed there for a few more moments, and as she felt a quickening, he stood and drove his cock into her. He gripped her hands and covered his mouth with hers. She began to tighten around him, and his pace increased. She broke the kiss to cry out, screaming out his name. And within seconds he came too, rearing back and calling out her name. He collapsed over her, breathing as heavily as she.

"Thank you for coming over. For coming back," he whispered into her neck.

She didn't know what to say. She didn't want to say anything for fear she would tear up. She smiled and wrapped her arms around his shoulders. And held him.

CHAPTER THIRTEEN

THE NEXT DAY, Andre had a day trip followed by days filled with meetings with people interested in hiring him as well as a big conference call regarding his Greenland trip.

Lauren would do her best to stay busy and not think about him. She had two meetings planned herself.

Her aunt's financial advisors requested a follow-up meeting with her for Tuesday. Then she planned to meet with Corinne.

Mr. Bernard sent a car in the morning, and they met in the conference room at his law office.

As they went over her aunt's impressive portfolio, it was clear, the advisors had clearly planned and invested well for her. They presented Lauren with the remaining paperwork needed to transfer the holdings to the US, information regarding Cole, their bank account numbers, and other tedious details.

Lauren fell silent for a moment. Her aunt had amassed such wealth, but she was no longer around to enjoy it. Lauren could only take comfort in believing that she enjoyed all she could while she could.

The real estate agent called to confirm their meeting later in the afternoon. The tone of Corinne's voice led her to believe that something wasn't running as smoothly as Corinne would have hoped. Lauren pressed her for details, but Corinne only said she would go over everything in person.

Promptly at four o'clock, Corinne walked into the restaurant and greeted Lauren with a kiss on each cheek. Lauren could certainly grow to like the European hospitality.

They chatted while bidding for the waiter, when Corinne started.

"Lauren, your aunt's house had been getting great showings, but they are slowing down. Drastically. I am very concerned that there are no offers as of yet. It's been over a week."

"You thought we would see some by now?"

"Yes," she replied. Then with poise and grace Lauren had become accustomed to seeing, she smoothed her lipstick and placed her hands in her lap. "I did a bit of asking around to see if I could learn what was prohibiting the offers. I'd hoped there was something that could be done to the house to enhance its marketability."

"Yes?" Lauren pulled her hand down as she realized she'd been playing with her necklace.

"It seems that your aunt enjoyed hosting parties at the house," Corinne raised her brows.

"Yes, I got a sense of that from her photos."

"Well," she paused as if searching for the right words, "it seems to be hindering the appeal of the house."

Lauren squinted her eyes. *Aunt Rosie's parties hindered the sale of the house?*

"How can I put this? Your aunt was gaining a reputation for being overly enthusiastic and maybe . . . decadent."

"I see. Well," Lauren glanced down at the table, "what do you suggest we do?"

"I will give it some more thought, but the first thing I can do, with your permission, is drop the price a bit. That might entice people to look beyond . . . the past. I will increase my marketing efforts as well."

"Okay. I like both of those ideas."

"I thought you might." Corinne slipped out a paper from her folder and presented it to Lauren. On the sheet, listed the new sales price.

It broke Lauren's heart. The house was beautiful. What a shame that "incentives" to buy were necessary when anyone would be lucky to have such a beautiful house in a desirable location.

She reviewed the document and signed it.

"I'll get this in the system and get the word out. I'll keep you apprised, Lauren."

"Thank you, Corinne."

Andre and Lauren met at a quaint restaurant for a late dinner that night. They ordered a variety of appetizers with a bottle of wine to share. He scooped up a scallop for her. Her lips curved and she closed her lips over the offering.

Andre took her hand and kissed her knuckles. "You look distracted. What's wrong, Lauren?"

She smiled and cupped her hand over his. "I have so much on my mind, that's all."

"Like what?"

"Well, my aunt's house for starters. My real estate agent said that showings are slowing down, and we have had no offers. She has a sense of urgency since I need to settle the estate as quickly as possible. But she believes there is something else going on."

"Something else?" He tilted his head slightly and looked so adorable, she wanted to reach over and kiss his lips hot.

"Well, she's concerned the house has a kind of reputation. Like perhaps all the parties my aunt threw were not well-received." She pursed her lips. "The house is lovely, but I think people are associating the house with my aunt."

"And since your aunt perhaps led a wild life, the house is somehow jinxed, yes?"

She nodded. "That's what the real estate agent thinks."

The waitress placed their appetizer in the middle of the table and refilled their wine glasses.

"Hmm," Andre furrowed his brows.

Lauren glanced at Andre and picked up her glass of wine for a sip.

"The house is very old, yes?"

"Yes. It was originally built in the sixteenth century, although modern updates have been made."

He nodded.

After several minutes, he broke the silence.

"Ah," he said with a smile creeping across his face. "What if you find out the *généalogie immobilière,* the history of the house? Maybe you will find something interesting, and people will then want to buy the house."

"Find out the history of the house?" she parroted. She didn't know where to begin a project like that.

"*Oui*. Get a look at the deed. It would give you the names of past owners. You could go to *Chambre départementale des notaires*. There are archives you could look at, and that could prove interesting."

She pushed a stray hair out of her face and licked her lips.

"That could work, Andre." She leaned toward him and placed a quick kiss on his lips. "I could find out about the house and publicize that and take the spotlight off my aunt and her reputation."

"*Exactement*," he said smiling back at her.

***

Lauren woke with determination. She had a quick breakfast and grabbed an apple and some snacks to shove in her bag to eat later. She had the feeling this would be a long day filled with old books and computer archives.

On Andre's advice, she started at the local notary, a rather modern building with a library feel. Her search was a grueling process since everything was in French. Several times she texted Andre, and he responded as timely as he could.

After most of the day spent finding nothing interesting, Lauren learned she needed to go to Tours, France where more archives were held. Probably information all the way back to the original owner.

She returned to the hotel and ordered room service. She shot Andre a text that she was back. Mere moments later he called.

"Hi."

"*Allô, chérie*. How did it go today?"

"Not bad, just not as productive as I'd hoped it might. I didn't learn too much except that the older archives are kept in Tours. So tomorrow I'm going there."

"Tours?"

"Well, yes. I can take the train. It's not very far."

"Aw, *chérie*. I wish I were there to take you myself."

"I know, but I'll be fine."

"Of course, you will."

His confidence in her made her smile.

"How are your meetings going?"

"Very well. I got a new job in Australia, but that won't start until September. How about we go out tomorrow for dinner?"

"That sounds great. If all goes as planned, I'll be on the three o'clock train back to Paris. I should be here by five-thirty."

"Great. I'll take my conference call from my hotel room and then drive back. Let's meet at L'Ecluse. I'll text you the address."

"Okay," she said and found herself grinning from ear to ear.

"I miss you. I can't wait to see you," he said in a low tone.

His words brought a warmth throughout her body. As if his words went from his mouth, through the phone and poured into her body.

It made her realize that likely most of their future conversations would be over the phone. She shook her head. Right now she didn't want to think about distance between them.

"What are you doing tonight?" he asked snapping her from her thoughts.

"I've ordered room service, then I'm taking a long bath and going to bed. I need to be at the train station early in the morning."

"Hmm. Perhaps you should call me when you are in the bath. Or even after your bath," he said with heat in his deep voice.

"My, Andre. What are you referring to?" she teased.

"I'm thinking I would talk to you about all the wonderful things I would like to do to you when I return. And I would love to hear you come over the phone with me."

Oh my.

"I would love to do that," she said softly, "but I should be good and go to bed." Although admittedly, she was already breathy with Andre's simple words. How she relished all the things he said to her, he did to her. How was she going to say goodbye to all that?

"I understand. Tomorrow then. But think of me, *chérie.*"

"I will, Andre," she smiled even though he couldn't see. "Good night."

"Sweet dreams, *ma chérie.*"

Lauren sighed as she set the phone on the bedside table. Andre was too good to her. She had become accustomed to talking to him and seeing him every day. They hadn't known each other very long, but she amazed herself at how quickly she'd grown closer to him. How she depended on him. She felt certain it had so much to do with being in a foreign country. With different language and customs, she needed the guidance of someone in the know.

Of course, that wouldn't explain why she didn't call on Mr. Bernard when she needed something.

Hmm. She sighed, and bit her bottom lip. It would be best if she realized Andre would not be in the U.S. when she returned, just as she could not stay in Paris. For him.

That would be crazy.

Andre lay on his hotel room bed in the dark thinking about Lauren, lying in her bed. Her pretty head laying on the pillow breathing smoothly, perhaps dreaming of him. He'd wish for that because he dreamed of her.

At times, he thought himself crazy for falling for a woman so soon. So damn soon after meeting. But there was something about her, and he simply could not pull away. In spite of himself, he knew she had to return to the States, yet he could not be away from her. Even now, in his hotel room, three hours away from Paris, he wanted to be with her.

Mon Dieu, what will he do once she leaves? How will he adjust? He shook his head. He didn't have the answers and thinking about it only depressed him further.

***

Lauren found herself in the reading room of the departmental archives in Tours. Over time, copies or originals of all documents relating to the transfer of property ownership found their way to Tours. And there was a lot there!

She combed through the documents looking for anything interesting that would help put her aunt's house in a positive light. She would retrieve the owner's name and in turn, look that up on the online database if she thought it sounded interesting. After hours of research, she found the usual stuff—doctors, lawyers, and an officer in the French Army—but mostly mundane facts.

Lauren wanted to cry. She was tired of sitting. Her eyes were tired, and she was almost to the beginning of the list of owners. There had to be something of interest somewhere here. She rubbed her eyes and continued to press on.

A name she pulled up showed something of interest. Possibly. She read about the original owner who had worked for the Sovereign Council.

She opened another screen to research the *Conseil Souverain*. The council made lasting changes in agriculture, commerce, the maintenance of public order, and sanitation. The board was formed at about the same time her aunt's house was built. Then, she saw it in front of her on the screen. The owner appeared to have been one of the original men appointed to the Council by King Louis the XIV. Could it be?

After she had reread it three more times, she printed the page and sought out the woman at the reference desk who spoke some English.

"Can you tell me, was this gentleman appointed by the King to his position?"

The woman read slowly and nodded as her eyes widen. She looked up at Lauren.

"Yes, he was selected to the *Conseil Souverain* by King Louis the Fourteenth," she said with her eyes smiling.

Incredible.

"Wow," Lauren said under her breath. "Thank you. May I get a copy of the deed?" She knew Corinne would want to see it.

After some effort, the woman presented her with a copy.

"Thank you," she said again and spun around to go back to the table where she worked. She had to tell Andre and Cole.

She shot a text to Andre first. She was so excited, she had to correct five typos before she could send it.

The original owner was appointed to the Conseil Souverain by King Louis XIV! I can't believe it!

Next she dialed Cole when she realized what time it was. *Crap!* She was going to miss her train. She scrambled to get her things together, throwing everything into her bag. She nearly ran out the front door to the train station. The station was a few blocks away, and if she ran, she might make it in time.

She didn't want to be late for getting back to Paris, for getting back to Andre.

She slowed her run long enough to navigate the stairs, and avoiding pedestrians, she sprinted on the platform right onto her train. She panted as she found a vacant seat and plopped down in it. *Geez, that was too close.* She heard the final announcement and felt the train lurch forward.

She leaned her head back on the seat back and took several deep breaths. As her breathing returned to normal, she sent off a text to Cole giving him a brief overview of what she learned. She bit on her bottom lip. She hoped the message went through because she could see the area had spotty cell service.

She laid her head against the headrest and closed her eyes. What a trying two days, but it had paid off. Lauren couldn't be happier.

When the train came into Paris proper, she sent an email to Corinne. She had snapped photos of the documents she'd gathered and sent those too. This *had* to be good news. This could be just what they needed to get her aunt's house sold.

CHAPTER FOURTEEN

LAUREN FOUND herself excited to see Andre again. Thrilled really. They were to rendezvous at L'Ecluse, a restaurant and bar on a side street, and a favorite of Andre's.

She returned to her hotel and had a few minutes to freshen up her makeup and run a brush through her hair before going down to take a cab to the restaurant.

She paid the cabbie and stepped out in front of the restaurant. A couple strolled out through the door hand in hand, and the man held open the door for Lauren. A million delectable scents from inside hit her olfactories and permeated her entire body.

"*Merci,*" she thanked the man.

As she walked through the entrance, she caught sight of Andre at the bar talking with a blonde woman. Lauren froze in her tracks. A beautiful blonde woman. And he was smiling at her. He placed his hand on her upper arm and leaned down to kiss her cheek.

Lauren's stomach seized. She couldn't move. She just stared at them. Andre rubbed the woman's arm and smiled at her again. She beamed at him. But of course she would; he was gorgeous.

The bubble Lauren was in burst in the few nanoseconds she watched Andre and the blonde. A man entered through the door behind Lauren and accidentally bumped into her. She hardly noticed.

"*Pardon*," he said and moved passed her.

As though Andre knew she was there, he looked over toward the door and saw her standing there. He smiled and waved to her. With only another moment evaporating, his face fell as he kept his eyes fixed on her. He frowned.

She managed to get her brain to function enough to tell her feet to move. To run. And that's what she did.

She spun around, almost bumping into two women that arrived, and bolted out the door. She heard her name being called. She took a right out the door and ran down the sidewalk.

"Lauren!" She heard Andre call her again, but she only ran faster. She would not let him see her cry.

She should have trusted her instinct. He was a fricking playboy. An asshole womanizer. *Sonofabitch!*

She ran not knowing where she was going. She just needed to get away from Andre and his pretty little playmate of the week. Out with the old, in with the new.

She felt one strong arm grab her waist. She shrieked. She spun around to look at him, tears welling in her eyes.

"Get away from me, you jerk! Asshole! How could you!"

She struggled to break free of his grasp, but now he had both arms wrapped around her, and he pulled her close to pin her body against his. The fury kept her standing when the pain in her heart would have made her collapse right there on the spot.

"Stop it," he scolded her. "Stop it. I will not let you manufacture some reason to run from me. I will not."

"What are you talking about? I saw you." Her voice raised, but now off the screaming volume so the passersby wouldn't think she was being attacked.

"What you saw, Lauren, was me congratulating an old friend. Tami worked for Paris Magazine when I shot for them some years ago. She and her husband are expecting their first child. She was waiting for him at the bar, drinking soda, when I saw her. I was simply congratulating her."

She stared at his face. Was he telling the truth? "You were?"

He nodded, and he moved his right arm up her back and grabbed a handful of her hair at her neck. He took a firm hold and plunged his lips down on hers in a heated, lustful kiss. His mouth claimed hers. Claimed her.

He broke the urgent kiss long enough to say, "You foolish girl. When will you learn?"

He backed her against a brick wall of a building and kissed her with ferocity and passion, the likes of which she'd never felt before. She wrapped her arms around his neck and pulled herself closer into his body.

"Learn what?" she breathed.

"That I'm in love with you, and I don't desire any other woman."

She pushed against his shoulders to separate their lips and allow her to see his eyes.

"No, Andre." He can't. He couldn't. She was leaving in eleven days. This was supposed to be a summer fling.

"Yes. *Absolument.* And I know you are leaving soon, but that does not change how I feel about you. I'm in love with you."

Her mouth gaped. They stared at each other, not uttering a word. He brought his other hand up her arm to her face. He smoothed stray hairs from her face.

"I'm helplessly in love with you, and I don't know what I'm going to do when you go," he said softly.

He brought his lips down to hers again in a more gentle way. He glossed his tongue over her lips and slipped it inside when she opened her mouth. She savored all the emotion he professed pour out into that kiss. The pain and disappointment that boiled inside mere minutes ago became a distant memory.

"Make love to me, Andre. Please. I don't want to wait another moment to feel you inside me," she whispered against his mouth.

He groaned. "*Ma chérie.*"

He took her hand, kissed the back of it and said, "Come with me."

They walked briskly, hand in hand down the street for three blocks, and turned right onto his street. As they walked, neither one spoke. Occasionally he would glance at her, and she would glance back at him.

After several minutes of walking, some of the initial heat she felt on the street started to dissipate, and in fact, the silence started to worry her. She should say something. She should apologize for being an imbecile. Again.

"Andre, I just want to say—"

"Don't."

Oh crap. He had time to think, and now he was angry. She most likely embarrassed him in front of a former co-worker. *Nothing worse than a jealous girlfriend acting like a five-year-old, right?* Not that they were boyfriend and girlfriend.

They walked up one flight of stairs to his apartment where he unlocked the door and followed her in.

"Are you mad at me?" she asked as the door closed.

In the blink of an eye, he threw the keys on the coffee table, scooped her up in his arms and marched to his bedroom.

She gasped.

"No," he said in a husky voice. Without warning, his lips came colliding down over hers for a lust-filled kiss. Clearly, the passion he felt on the street had *not* subsided.

He set her on her feet beside his bed, and yanked his t-shirt up over his head. Next, he grabbed the hem of her shirt out of her pants and tugged, pulling it off. A faint plink sounded across the room that might have been a ricochet button.

He reached for her head, cupped her face and drew her closer to him, staring straight into her eyes. He leaned his head down to kiss her gently on the lips as if he were trying to slow the pace. He wrapped one arm around her waist and pulled her closer still. She could feel his erection against her belly. She moved her hands up his strong arms and shoulders to the back of his head and wove her fingers through his hair. The kiss grew more passionate and urgent as he slowly slid his hand down to caress her behind. She moaned into his mouth as his big warm hand fondled her, kneaded her.

Andre broke the kiss and skimmed his hands up her belly to her breasts. He slowly rubbed both his thumbs over her nipples tucked in her lacy bra, and brought them more taut and pointed. Her breasts grew heavy.

He lowered his mouth, kissed and licked her neck and chest slowly and sensuously. He slipped her bra straps off her shoulders and brought his mouth to her now-exposed nipples. He took one nipple in his mouth, sucked gently and teased with his tongue.

"Oh," she sighed. The moisture pooled at the apex of her thighs and the ache began to build.

"*Magnifique.* I worship your beautiful breasts."

And he did. He reached behind her and unhooked her bra letting it fall to the floor. He cupped her breasts in his two warm hands and took a hardened nipple in his mouth. He moved to the other one, sucking and tugging. Then blew a breath over them causing her to moan.

Undoing her pants button and zipper, he crouched down and took her pants with him. She placed her hands on his shoulders and stepped out. Still down low, he brought his mouth to her stomach to kiss, lick, and nibble. He moved lower and kissed her through her lacy panties. She moaned.

His hands slid up her legs, snatched her panties and pulled them down. She stepped out of them, returning her legs to a wider stance.

He caressed his index finger over her sex and tested her wetness. She moaned again and let her head drop back.

"Turn around and place your hands on the bed."

She hesitated only a fraction of a second because, while there were no lights on in his bedroom, the light from outside poured in through his window blinds. But the throbbing at her sex beat down the shyness of the exposed and vulnerable position she'd be in. She did as he bid. She faced the bed and placed her hands on the mattress.

Although she couldn't see him, Lauren heard Andre take off his pants and underwear and fish out a condom, which he flung on the bed beside her.

He leaned over her naked body, whispering in French in her ear. She only wished she understood those sweet nothings. As he moved his lips down her back, kissing and licking, he smoothed his hands down the back of her thighs. He blew on her spine sending a shiver rippling out.

"Spread your legs for me, *chérie*." His hands caressed her thighs inside and outside. Up and down. His warm hands sent tantalizing tingles all over.

She was dripping now. The ache in her swollen sex practically intolerable.

"Andre, please."

He continued his kisses on her behind while bringing his hands up the inside of her thighs to her sex. Gingerly he stroked her slick lips coating her swollen clit. She moaned and writhed at his touch. Her orgasm lingered under the surface. She pushed back on his hands, but he pulled them away, not giving her the stimulation she desperately needed.

"You feel so good, *chérie*. Breathe. I promise to make you feel good."

She inhaled deeply, and he brought his fingers back to tantalizing her sex again, but never entering her wet channel.

The lack of blood to her brain caused a delay, but she figured it out. He used some kind of Kama Sutra on her to draw out her orgasm. He wasn't letting her settle for the mini-explosions when the gigantic climax could be so much more.

"Down on your elbows, *chérie*," he whispered.

She lowered to her forearms effectively exposing her whole backside and sex to him. She felt his warm breath *there*.

"Oh," she breathed.

Her heart beat hard against her chest; she panted. His tongue slowly massaged her clitoris as he danced his fingers around her swollen lips. The whole blessed area was one pile of sensitized nerves. One more right move and she'd detonate.

As if reading her mind, that is just what he did. With his tongue swirling over her clit, he slipped two fingers inside her, twirled them and pumped them. She released with an explosion of sensation that damn-near made her pass out. She screamed his name, not realizing how loud it might have been.

Andre managed to roll on a condom with one hand, slid his fingers out, and plunged into her tight channel. He let out a groan.

His cock in her felt warm and filled her perfectly.

"Oh God, Andre."

"Yes, *chérie*. I will make love to you all night. Every night. I will get my fill of you and you of me."

He panted in her ear, kissing her neck as he continued his controlled pump.

"Andre, you're perfect."

She could feel another climax building. Impossible, after the one she just had!

Andre pulled back, short-stroked her and stimulated her first few inches. *Sweet Jesus!* Tears leaked from the corners of her eyes.

"Oh, baby. Don't stop." She clutched the sheets while the orgasm began its slow climb. He pumped faster in her, and as she cried out, he spilled himself inside her, growling her name as he came.

Together they collapsed on the bed, panting, basking in the glow of another amazing orgasm.

After their breathing had returned mostly to normal, he pulled out and rolled off to the side of her.

She lay for a moment flashing back to the events that brought them to this point. She felt compelled to explain herself. To apologize. This was the second time jealousy had flashed its ugly head with Andre.

Lauren had boyfriends before and never considered herself a jealous person. Now, she counted two different instances in which she felt a gut reaction about Andre and women. What was wrong with her?

"Andre, I'm sorry about what happened in the restaurant. I jumped to conclusions about the woman I saw you with."

He turned his head to look at her.

"I think I was jealous," She trailed off, not really sure what she was feeling then or how to articulate it now. "I'm not sure where that comes from." Her brows pinched together.

"In a way, I liked that you were jealous," he spoke softly. "But when I saw you run, I panicked. Seeing you leave tore my heart out, Lauren."

Her heart clenched at his words. She glanced down.

"I'm not mad." He lifted her hand to his mouth and kissed the inside of her wrist. "I suspect some of this stems from losing your parents so young."

She nodded in contemplation. "I don't mean to push you away, Andre. I don't mean to," she closed her eyes, "to sabotage our relationship." She felt tears form in her eyes because it occurred to her that that was what she was doing—sabotaging their relationship. And he was so incredibly patient and understanding about it. "I'm afraid of what I feel for you," she whispered.

He gently kissed her. "I know it is too early to tell you, but I said it, and I meant it. I love you. I know you care about me, too. We have only a limited amount of time together, and I want to capture all of it and savor it."

God, he had such a way with words. How could she refuse him anything? She didn't want to think about their time remaining. She didn't want to think about going home. Without him. She would do what he said. Spend what time they had together and savor every moment of it.

CHAPTER FIFTEEN

LAUREN CAREFULLY folded a new sundress in her suitcase and zipped the case closed. That should do it.

Butterflies filled her stomach as she gathered her purse and sunglasses. Andre would be at her hotel door in a few minutes, and they would be off for the weekend. She relished her time with Andre. They had spent the entire day together the day before.

She smiled in recollection. He warmed her from the inside out. He brought out a freshness and appreciation for life that Lauren hadn't even realized she'd been missing. Andre had changed her, and for that, she would always be thankful.

Her cell phone rang, interrupting her thoughts, Cole. *Crap.* She hadn't spoken to him in days, and he had tried to call her yesterday.

"Hello?" she answered.

"Lauren. It's Cole."

"Hi, Cole. How are you?"

"Never mind that. How are you?" His voice sounded stern. She shouldn't be surprised.

"I'm good. Busy. The house is getting some showings, but no offers. I think I found some interesting history that the real estate agent can use." She took a breath and let the other shoe drop. "And Andre asked me to come on a business trip with him, so I'm packing right now."

The phone line was silent.

"Lauren, do you think that's a good idea?"

"Sure. The real estate agent has everything under control. There's not much I can do at this point, and I want to see some of the Continent before coming home."

"Continent?" he almost yelled. "Where the hell are you going?"

"Just Croatia. Andre needs to photograph the Brela Beach. It was listed on Forbes as a Top Ten."

"So, when will you be back?" he asked in a calmer voice. He referred to returning to New York, not Paris. Lauren swallowed hard. She wanted to stay longer. Stay with Andre.

"Well, I . . . I wanted to talk to you about that. I may go with Andre to Pamplona, Spain for the San Fermin festival."

"The running of the bulls? When is that?"

"It starts on July sixth."

"Christ, Lauren." So much for calm.

"I know," her voice full of regret. "If you don't want me to go, I'll understand. I haven't even spoken to Regina about staying longer. How is she anyway?"

Cole let out a long exhale. "She's her usual self. Look, do you mind if I sleep on it. Give it some thought."

Her lips curved slightly.

"Sure, let's talk later," she said feeling more hopeful. "I'll call you when I get back from Croatia."

"Okay. Be careful please."

"I will. Love you."

"Love you back," she disconnected the line.

***

Andre boarded the plane for Croatia with Lauren right in front of him. He lifted her bag into the overhead baggage compartment and sat down beside her.

After they had buckled, he took her hand and kissed her knuckles. He always enjoyed holding her hand.

"Are you excited?"

She twisted toward him and let her smile grow.

"Yes. Very. I'm excited about what I learned about my aunt's house this week. I'm looking forward to getting to the beach and seeing more of Europe before I have to head home."

He saw her smile waver slightly. He knew she didn't like to think about going back to the U.S. any more than he did, and that slip seemed to take her by surprise.

"Have you been to Croatia before?" she continued.

"I have not, so it will be new for me too."

The flight was reasonably short, and after one stopover, they landed at an airport several miles from their hotel.

In the cab, he retrieved the travel information from his bag.

"There are a few things we can see while we're here," he glanced down.

"Yeah? More than just beach?" she teased.

He peeked a look her way and smiled.

"*Oui*. There is an iconic rock, an old church, and we can do some shopping at the outdoor market. And I've heard Croatian food is excellent." He had a few other ideas of things they would do, but he would let that be a surprise.

"Great," she said with a twinkle in her eye.

The drive to the hotel at first seemed much like any other country in Europe, but as they got closer to the hotel and the beach, the view became much more scenic.

"Oh, Andre. Look at how lush and green everything is. It's positively beautiful," Lauren gushed.

Checking in and finally entering their hotel room, Lauren was giddy with excitement. He loved seeing her this way. Happy, relaxed, not thinking about going back to New York.

Their hotel room didn't appear overly grand, but truly with the amazing view of the ocean, it wasn't necessary. There were some quaint touches, like a wooden writing desk in the corner, window niches, and a copper bathing tub that made it feel cozy.

Lauren's eyes lit up at the view out the window. A vast blue ocean outlined with sandy beach interspersed with rocky alcoves. She meandered out to the balcony and drew in a breath.

"Oh, Andre. This is beautiful. I want to walk along the beach tonight. Can we?"

He stepped behind her and placed his hands over hers. Her skin felt soft and warm to his touch.

"*Oui. Absolument*," he leaned down to brush away the hair from her neck and gently kiss her tender skin. He felt her shiver, and he grinned.

"What do you have to do first?"

He sighed. She referred to his work taking photographs as he was contracted to do. He had a list of shots he needed to get during their few-day respite. Of course, he almost always gave the client more than what they asked, and he wanted to start that night.

"Let's change and head to the concierge. There are rocky parts to this beach. I want to know the best way to move around and make sure we stay safe."

"Okay."

In a flash, Lauren had her baggage opened, unpacked, and she'd changed into shorts and sandals as he requested. He chuckled softly at her enthusiasm for the beach, for their new adventure.

On location, Andre combed a few good eastern-facing spots for the early morning. He snapped a few test shots as they walked hand in hand and took in the surroundings.

Lauren carried her sandals, and although she wore sunglasses, he could tell her eyes were smiling. He didn't resist snapping photos of his beautiful *chérie* at any opportunity. He would want them for later. When she was gone, and he was alone to do nothing but think of all they shared during their very short time together.

He hated thinking about it. He scrubbed his hand over his face. He already knew he would be miserable without her. And although they promised to see each other, he knew the chance of that happening with any reasonable frequency was unrealistic.

"Hey," Lauren cried out, pulling him from his melancholy. "I think that's the rock you mentioned."

Sure enough, several meters ahead of them, and a small distance offshore, a large rock with a tree and some brush growing on it lay in the water. As they got closer, he could see that no one was on it. Perhaps it was too jagged, too dangerous. He scouted nearby areas and cliffs that would provide the right angles for the best shots.

After more than two hours of walking and shooting, they returned to their hotel room to get ready for dinner. He was thankful for the air conditioning because Croatia was certainly hotter than Paris at this time of the year.

They freshened up. As Lauren readied herself in the bathroom, Andre strolled to the balcony and stared out at the beautiful sight before him, so tranquil and inviting. *Perhaps I can make this an extra special night for* ma chérie, he thought. And a slow, mischievous smile spread across his lips.

Lauren opted for a cotton summer dress—fitted on top and flowing on the bottom. She bought it in Paris, and it was quickly becoming one of her favorites. Not only because it felt soft and cool, but because the look in Andre's sparkling eyes told her she looked good in it.

He sent out a low, slow whistle.

"Let's call room service," he said in a husky voice as he cleared his throat.

She stepped to him and let his arms wrap around her.

"No way, mister. I want to you to take me into town tonight." She stood on tip-toes and kissed his lips. "You will not keep me locked up in this room, and have your wicked way with me," she scolded. "Yet."

He gave her a full-on smile, letting the dimple that she loved so much show.

"All right. Fair enough. Dinner in town."

They walked hand-in-hand for three blocks and came upon the quaint, bustling restaurant the hotel concierge had recommended.

The scent filling the air around the restaurant was mouth-watering. Despite the crowd, they were shown to a lovely table by a window. Lauren couldn't decide what to order. It all looked so fascinating and good. She exhaled.

"What are you getting, *chérie*?"

"I don't know," she bit her lower lip. "How about you?"

"I think I will try the *cevapcici*."

Lauren had considered that because it seemed most like meatballs, and she liked meatballs.

"Okay, I have an idea. My other choice was the *buzara* with the fish. So you get *cevapcici,* and we can try each other's dishes. Okay?"

His gorgeous mouth curved upward. "Sounds good to me."

The waiter delivered them each a glass of wine, and Andre held his up for a toast.

"To you, my lovely *chérie*. And to our wonderful escape together."

She smiled and clinked glasses with him. *Yes, to their wonderful escape.* If Cole wasn't keen on letting her stay longer to travel to Spain with Andre, she needed to get back to New York on time. Therefore, this would be their last full weekend together. She would enjoy every single moment she could.

After a wholly satisfying, delicious dinner, they meandered through town, peered into shops, and admired the wares through the store windows. The throng of people had thinned now that it got dark.

Andre took her hand, kissed her knuckles and said, "Let's go walk along the beach."

"I would love to," she said with a twinkle in her eye. He was quickly coming to love that twinkle.

Arriving at the beach, they slipped off their shoes and held them while they strolled along the soft sand. Only a few people could be seen at this time of night, which pleased Andre for he had hopes of finding a secluded spot to be alone with his *chérie*.

As they chatted, Andre kept track of their location, remembering where they had been from earlier that day. He led them in a direction away from most of the hotels. He spied a small alcove protected by a rock formation with a clear view of the Adriatic. Even though there were few people on the beach that night, the location would be private, and that was most important to Andre.

When they arrived at their destination, he asked, "Shall we sit for a while?"

Thoughts of Lauren filled his mind all day. Seeing her long, lean legs in her shorts, her playful smiles and her kissable mouth only made focusing on work more of a challenge.

Not that he was bothered by that. He loved having her along on his trip. So often, he traveled alone and worked alone. This was a treat on many levels.

She took a seat beside him and hooked her arm through his.

"I hope you don't mind getting a little sandy," he said.

"Not at all. It's quite lovely out here. Peaceful, and I don't think I have ever seen quite so many stars."

She was correct. Being away from big cities with their million lights, it seemed one could spy every possible star.

"I am so glad you agreed to come on this trip with me."

She tipped her head and smiled at him. "Me too."

He leaned in and placed an easy little kiss on her cheek and with his index finger, he guided her head to face him. He kissed her luscious lips and trailed down her neck. He felt her tremble. He brushed her hair aside and kissed her slow and easy, letting his tongue dance along her skin.

She sighed.

He drew back and stretched out his legs and held her hand while he gave a gentle tug. "Come here. Sit on my lap, *chérie*," he cajoled.

Her dark eyes met his, she hesitated briefly and did as he asked. She swung one leg over his legs and rested on his thighs.

His arms tightened around her waist and pulled her closer. She mewled when she came flush against his growing erection. He pulled her close for a kiss. He could feel her full, warm lips and gentle tongue coaxing his to play.

He broke the kiss only enough to move to her silky neck. He kissed and nipped as he moved to her shoulder and slipped a dress strap off her shoulder. "You look beautiful tonight, *chérie*. I love this dress on you."

"Thank you," she whispered in throaty tone.

He knew he was making her wet. He loved making her feel good. He leisurely slid a hand along her thigh, slipping under her dress and stopping at her panty line. He traced a finger along its edge.

"*Chérie*, have you ever come on a sandy beach?" he breathed into her neck.

She shook her head because words were too much effort at that moment.

"No? I would like to fix that."

One finger slipped under her satin panty line to her lush swollen pussy. *Mon Dieu!* She was incredibly wet. Wet and ready for him. But he would not rush this astonishing night for her.

He caressed her plump, wet lips slowly finding his way to her hard little nub. Her eyes drifted closed. She gripped his shoulders and gently rocked against him. He knew what she wanted because he was desperate for it too.

"*Chérie*, have you ever made love on a sandy beach?" and with that, he drove a finger up into her wet channel.

She moaned and let her head fall back.

He had his answer. "No? We shall need to fix that."

But now, his cock swelled to its maximum and pressed painfully against his slacks. He needed to reposition himself.

He pulled out his finger and nearly lost it when her eyes flew open, her head straightened, and she squeaked, "What are you doing?"

He bit back a smile. "No worry. I'm making more room for both of us." He shifted her back several inches and undid his button and zipper, freeing his cock.

"That's better." He exhaled. "Now, let me pull those pretty panties off you."

She gave a shy smile and rose to let him remove them. Her beautiful pussy was mere inches from his face. He grabbed her waist and placed a quick kiss over her dress directly on her sweet spot before she returned to his lap. How he'd wanted her to stand and lift her dress, but that would be too much for her.

He dove back into her mouth with his mouth and moaned as she unabashedly reached her gentle hands to his cock. She moaned.

He broke the kiss and heard her panting. He reached into a pocket and retrieved a condom. She took it but didn't cover him as he expected. Instead, she scooted back on his legs, and wrapping her fingers around his cock, she leaned forward and licked and sucked him into her warm, wet mouth. He groaned.

She worked her tongue and lips in time with her fist, up and down. He let his head drop back to savor the delicious pleasure she gave him.

"*Chérie*, please stop. When I come, I want to be inside you."

She looked up at him and blinked. She rose upright and covered him with the condom.

He pulled her closer and plunged his tongue into her beautiful, talented mouth.

With a grip on her hips, he said, "On your knees, *cherie*. You can hold my shoulders. I'm going to give you an amazing orgasm under the stars. Then I will dive inside you and do it again."

Her mouth parted, and she nodded. She grasped his shoulders and rose from his lap, balancing on her knees and shins.

His hands left her waist and glided down her hips and thighs to beneath her dress. He slowly inched upward with splayed hands, rubbing over little drops of moisture that had trickled down.

With light, teasing strokes, his fingers played with her sex, and her hips convulsed. He didn't stop. He wanted her to have the perfect orgasm. He knew what would do just that.

With her breasts mere inches from his mouth, he released one hand and slid it around her back. He groaned as his hand cupped her delicious ass. He could not be distracted. He pushed her, so her breasts came flush to his face. He immediately kissed them over the dress, and he licked her décolletage. Her moan was like music to his ears.

"I want your breasts, *chérie*. Please," he whispered.

She looked down at him, blinked, and one strap at a time, she lowered her dress enough to give him her bare breasts. He groaned. And without hesitation he took one peaked, long nipple into his mouth and sucked.

She cried out but didn't pull away. She grabbed locks of hair at the back of his head. He licked the areola and continued to suck. Her head fell back, and she arched farther into his mouth. He tongued one nipple and the other, all the while, stroking and playing with her sex.

Slowly he slid a finger inside her, and she moaned. He pulsed in and out, and he added a second finger.

"Andre," she breathed.

He wouldn't go fast. Not now. He wanted her so addicted to him, to his orgasms, to his lovemaking.

And no distance—nothing—would matter when she needed to be with him again. He would make it so good, she would never forget him.

"You are beautiful, *cherie*. I love you. I love to see you come," he inserted a third finger and pumped only fractionally faster. Then he twisted inside her, and he felt the first tightening of her inner muscles. He returned his mouth to her breasts and sucked each nipple, bringing another clenching of her sex. Without warning, he drove his fingers all the way in, sucked hard on a nipple.

Her orgasm hit her full-force, and she cried out his name. He felt her muscles pull in his fingers, and he pumped inside her a few more times before he took her hips and pulled her down. As she came down over him, he thrust deep inside. Her hands gripped his shoulders with passion and screamed as he continued to pump into her.

"God, Andre," she panted.

He held her tight and moved her body over his. She cupped his face and brought her lips to his to another long, searing kiss. They kissed and moaned and moved as one. Regardless of where she lived, she would always be his.

"*Chérie*," he breathed against her lips.

"Andre, I'm close," she groaned.

"What do you need, *chérie*? Touch yourself." She leaned back and met his eyes. "Let me see you touch yourself and bring yourself to orgasm."

She did not protest. She took her right hand off his shoulder, pulled her dress out of the way, and smoothed her finger over her clit. Her eyelids lolled closed.

He released his hold on her and leaned back on his elbows and watched. She was a sight, a rare beauty. His beauty. He fervently focused his energy on not coming until she did. He pulsed his hips inside her and heard her moan. Her finger moved faster.

Then it happened. Andre watched his *belle chérie* ride him and her finger to an explosive orgasm. Her face flushed, she whimpered, writhed, and let out a low scream. She looked amazing. The sight of his love on top of him would stay with him until the day he died.

As she came down from her high, Andre swung them both around to have her lay beneath him. He dove into her and released what he had been holding in all day.

"I love you, Lauren," he panted into her neck.

She clasped her arms and legs around him and held tightly. They lay on the beach together with him inside her for several minutes.

Later, in silence, they dressed to head back to the hotel.

They showered and made unhurried love one last time. He buried his nose in her hair and inhaled her scent. She nestled her body into his as they fell asleep in each other's arms. Nothing would ever come close to how it felt to make love to Lauren on the beach tonight, he thought. Nothing.

CHAPTER SIXTEEN

LAUREN AWOKE to Andre's kisses down her bare back. Within seconds, he had her wet and ready. Lauren had never experienced love making like this.

She sighed.

Last night on the beach was nothing short of outstanding. Her heart was full. His kiss was more than a prelude to sex. She could feel the emotion pouring out of him and touching her like never before. She thought she'd been in love before, but it never felt like this. So all-consuming and fulfilling. What she felt for Andre somehow brought about a peace and satisfaction she hadn't even realized she'd been missing.

Andre had changed something in her. Forever.

Sitting on the balcony overlooking the sea, Lauren sipped on her coffee as she waited for Andre to return from his early shooting. Out of the blue, the thought struck her. She'd been too excited about her trip with Andre, she forgot to turn on her phone the previous day after they had landed. She grinned and shook her head at her absent-mindedness.

As she powered on her phone, Andre strolled in. He didn't bother to say hello. He crossed to the table, set down his camera bag and cupped her face bringing his lips to hers for a heated tongue kiss.

After several moments, he broke away and smiled down at her.

"Well, good morning, *Monsieur* Beauchamp."

"I missed you," he said in the rich, deep voice he had. "Care to join me in a shower?"

"I had better not. I forgot to power on my phone yesterday and I think I have messages."

"Okay, *chérie*." He placed a chaste kiss on her lips and whispered, "Next time." He pointed a finger her way and gave her a sexy little wink before heading to the bathroom.

Mmm, she thought to herself as she watched him. Her man was delicious.

Lauren glanced down and saw messages left by Regina, her boss, and Cole.

Her phone rang in her hand, and she jumped in surprise. Regina. *What is going on?*

"Hello?"

"Lauren. This is Regina. I've been trying to get a hold of you since yesterday."

"I'm sorry. I'm in Croatia and my phone was off."

She heard Regina's loud exhale. "Yes, I heard. Probably better that I hadn't spoken to you yesterday because I was positively fuming. I received an anonymous letter stating that Colton is straight. Did you know that?"

Oh no! "About the letter?" Her heart beat rapidly in her chest.

"No. About your brother," she snipped, but not waiting for an answer, she continued. "Of course you did. It was probably your idea. Well, I need you to get back here to the States immediately. I fired Colton."

She gasped. "Regina, I'm don't know what happened, and I'm very sorry about this. I thought—"

"I know what you thought," cutting her off. "Do you understand how vulnerable you've left the spa because of this stunt? My attorneys are scrambling to try to mitigate the damage. Letters are going out to the entire staff and clientele in an attempt to stave off any lawsuits."

Oh God.

Regina repeated that she needed her to return to New York or be out of a job.

As she hung up, Andre stepped out of the shower. For a split second, she forgot about her world crashing around her when the most beautiful man with warm, sparkling brown eyes smiled at her.

His smile quickly fell when he saw her dazed face. He tied his towel tighter around his waist and crossed to Lauren. The color in her face faded.

"*Chérie*, what is it?"

"My employer called from New York." She swiped her tongue over her upper lip several times and furrowed her brows. "Andre, please sit. I need to tell you something."

They both sat on the sofa, and instinctively he reached to hold her hand.

"The spa where I work in New York is very exclusive and unique. It's a female-only spa, and the clientele is not always required to wear clothing."

He cocked an eyebrow. "Interesting."

"Yes. So in order to come here, I needed to have someone fill in and manage the spa for me. I have my brother doing that."

Andre tipped his head, trying to figure out how that might work.

"He is pretending to be gay," answering his unspoken question.

"You're kidding?"

"No. Well, somebody found out and sent an anonymous letter to my employer. Needless to say, she was upset." She glanced down, and he saw her lip quiver. She looked up with sad eyes. "She fired my brother and told me to come back immediately or I would be fired, too."

Tears welled in her eyes. Andre took her other hand in his, waited for her to continue, but at the same time not wanting to hear what she was bound to say.

"I need to go back as soon possible," she whispered.

Andre shored every gram of strength to remain still and not tell Lauren to tell her employer where to shove it. He held her gaze. Supporting Lauren now was more important than his selfish needs.

"Whatever you think is best," he nodded.

"Oh, Andre. I don't know what's best," she pleaded. "The house hasn't sold. How can I leave with so many loose ends? Not to mention, we still had a whole week left to be together." Tears streamed down her lovely cheeks.

He smoothed her tears away with his thumb. "Shh, *chérie*. It will be all right." He pulled her close to wrap his arms around her. Would it be alright?

She sniffled.

"Whatever you need, I'm here for you, *chérie*."

She slipped back from his hold, and meeting his gaze, she breathed, "I need to call my brother."

"*Oui*." He nodded, kissed the top of her head, and retreated to the bath to give her privacy.

As he finished getting ready, all he could think about was how this had happened. A bittersweet smile crossed his face. He knew. His Lauren was creative and a risk-taker. She would try anything once.

Unfortunately, it appeared her plan blew up. It blew up in New York and had spread to Paris. *Merde*! He had hoped they could stay in Croatia an extra day, but that seemed to be impossible. He exhaled hard, and leaning both hands on the counter, he dropped his head. How much time did they have left?

She picked up the phone and dialed her brother. She informed him that she'd already heard from Regina, which Cole wasn't too happy about.

"What are you going to do?" he asked.

"Hell if I know, Cole. The house hasn't sold, and it needs my attention. But I can't be at two places at once." She realized how ridiculous she sounded stating the obvious. "What happened?" she furrowed her eyebrows.

"I don't know." He sighed audibly. "Lauren, I am sorry. I fucked up, and I know it."

"Cole, there's nothing we can do about it now. I need to talk to the real estate agent and come up with a plan." She let out an exasperated sigh. "Just so you know, Regina sent out a letter to the clientele telling them about the situation and how everything was under control since you are no longer working for the spa. Also, she told me she spoke to her attorneys. She's, of course, concerned about lawsuits."

"Shit."

"Ya' got that right," she said with sarcasm. She took a calming breath. "I need to think on it.

You'll probably be picking me up from the airport in a few days."

The thought of which broke her heart in two. Her time with Andre would be cut short. Tears welled in her eyes.

"Okay. Keep me posted," Cole said, and without saying a word, she hung up.

She sank into a chair; her phone gripped in her hand so tight her knuckles turned white. Her nostrils flared as she glared down at her phone. She fumed. She was so mad she wanted to punch something. Mad and hurt. What the hell went wrong? *How could he let this happen?*

She shook her head. She chided herself for being rude to her brother. No forgiveness. No goodbye. She took her anger out on Cole, and chances were it wasn't intentional. Her eyes closed and several tears streamed down her cheeks. She didn't see Andre walk into the room.

He crossed to the table where she sat.

"Are you all right?"

She glanced up at him and shook her head.

"Not really, but what can I do?"

"I'll call the airline and get our flight changed to later today."

"Oh, Andre. I am so sorry. No. If you need to stay and work, I can go back by myself." She felt the tears of frustration threatening.

He took a hold of her hand to calm her.

"Lauren, I was up early and got some excellent shots. Let me see how today goes. We can either leave tonight or first thing in the morning, okay?"

Her lips pressed together and she nodded her head. He placed a kiss on her cheek and rose to evaluate his camera bag and supplies.

She fought back the tears. He was so kind to her that her heart ached. She ungraciously wiped her nose with the back of her hand. She felt like a hot mess. She was overly emotional and moody. One minute rude, the next minute vulnerable.

She froze. *Oh God.*

She opened an app on her phone that tracks her cycle. There it was in blue and white. She bit her lip, her period was due. No wonder her emotions were all over the board.

Snapping her out of her haze, Andre looked her way and said, "Would you like to come with me?"

What were her options? Stay and mope, boiling over with hurt and anger over the fiasco in New York? Or, go with handsome Andre and enjoy a Sunday afternoon in a country to which she may never return?

"Give me a few minutes, and I'll be ready." The smile on Andre's lips told her she made the right decision. She grabbed her shorts and t-shirt and bolted for the bathroom.

Andre took many more pictures and captured several with the sunset. He climbed up the side of a small cliff and levered himself to get a shot facing up the beach with the breathtaking view.

"Please be careful," Lauren called in a shaky voice.

She was nervous for him, but sometimes the risk was well worth the reward. It may have been precarious, but it was worth it. He knew his client would be thrilled by what he had on his camera.

They walked, and his work seemed to distract Lauren to the point where she looked more relaxed. But more than once, Andre glanced her way and found her looking solemn and distant. He couldn't blame her. She devised a plan that would allow her to attend to her aunt's estate out of the country, meanwhile maintaining a thriving business for her employer. And the whole situation erupted.

He felt for her, for her whole predicament she now faced.

He had a lot of respect for her. She was keeping it all together.

They held hands as they walked along the beach, shared a quiet dinner and retired early because they had the first flight out in the morning.

He wanted to make love to her that night, but she told him she was too uncomfortable on the first day of her cycle and would rather not. He understood completely.

He wrapped his arms around her and held her while she slept. He wished he could fix what went wrong, but that was unrealistic. All he could do was comfort her.

In the back of his mind lay the nagging question—what of them? What of him?

***

Late Monday, she met with the real estate agent to check on the progress of selling her aunt's house.

"The information you sent last week has been

tremendous for your aunt's house. Showings have spiked. I am very pleased with the feedback I am receiving about the house."

In a seemingly uncharacteristic move, Corinne placed both hands over Lauren and let out a full-blown smile.

"I am certain you will be receiving offers any day now."

Lauren gave a half-smile because that was all she could muster.

"What is wrong, Lauren? You don't look pleased."

She sighed. "Corinne, I need to go back to the States right away. Something demands my attention there. If there is a way, will we be able to close long-distance or via proxy?"

Corinne straightened and furrowed her brow a fraction.

"I'm sorry you have to go so soon. I believe what you ask is possible. I will look into it and let you know. When are you leaving?"

Her throat constricted. "The day after tomorrow," she managed to get out.

"I see. Tomorrow, I'll call you with the details on how to proceed."

"Thank you."

"And thank you." She paused momentarily, "Best of luck, Lauren."

She forced a smile, when in fact she was dying inside. Her world crashed around her.

CHAPTER SEVENTEEN

LAUREN THOUGHT back to her flight over to Paris and how excited she was about the trip. Since then, everything had changed, in a few short weeks. She endured the emotional rollercoaster of clearing out her aunt's house and fell in love with the most amazing man. The perfect man for her.

You had to go home eventually.

Her heart ached at the thought of being without Andre. She wiped the tears from her face and began packing.

That night Andre made dinner for her, and they lounged in front of the TV afterward. Very few words were said. What could they say?

The next day, their last day together, he told her to stay with him.

She called Mr. Bernard to verify next steps to follow once she was back in the States. She also had arranged for her storage unit to be cleared, and the contents sent home.

Lauren realized she hadn't shown Andre, her aunt's house, so she invited him to see it.

They meandered through the house and stopped in each room.

"The house is *magnifique*," he murmured into her hair as he kissed her head.

"It is, isn't it? Being in this house gives me a feeling of what my aunt was like. And because of that, it makes me feel closer to my mother," she looked up and smiled. A real smile, even if it was small.

"What was she like?"

Lauren swallowed. "She had a good heart. She saw the good in everyone. She was full of life. Both my parents were. My dad was firm but in a loving way. He rarely raised his voice to us kids." She sighed. "I'd like to think that one day I might have the chance to parent as they had. As lovingly as they had."

The melancholy of knowing this would be their last day together for a while weighed heavily on them. Andre touched her constantly. They ate lunch at an outdoor deli, even though neither of them was hungry.

She looked up from her salad.

"Andre, it will be hard."

"*Chérie*, I know, but I don't care. I will come visit you as often as I can. We will meet in new places. We will seek every opportunity to be together," he gave her a small smile.

A few tears escaped and streamed down her cheeks. She nodded. He reached over to wipe away the tears from her cheeks and kiss her forehead.

She knew it would be hard. Insanely hard for them to see each other with any regularity.

They walked the city streets for another hour before heading back to his place. With few words, he poured them each a glass of white wine, took her hand and led her to the bedroom. Gingerly they undressed each other, slowly savoring every glide over their skin. He murmured French softly in her ear, and she stroked her fingertips over his muscular body.

The lovemaking was slow and sensual, like they had a lifetime to learn each other's bodies from top to bottom and back up again. They made love several times before dozing off for two hours. He woke her, and they made love until the sun came up.

"*Je t'aime*," he whispered over and over.

He had her laid out on the bed to kiss, suck and nip at her entire body. He had her wrapped tightly around him under the covers moving slowly, bringing her to orgasm after orgasm.

Every cell, every nerve, in tune with him. They moved as one. Never thinking about the future, only the here and now. Until finally, the time had come.

"Andre, I need to get ready."

He froze. After a beat, he nodded and helped her to the shower. He drove her to the hotel to retrieve her bags and finalize the hotel bill. The nausea in her stomach grew with each passing minute. She was certain he felt the same way. Several times she fought back tears.

Her heart ached at the thought of leaving Andre.

People bustled around them at De Gaulle Airport, and Lauren could hardly focus on anything but Andre. She was needed back in New York. She desperately held back the tears brimming in her eyes. The spa needed her. Her brother needed her. She'd gone over this a thousand times. *So make your feet move toward the gate.*

With her ticket in one hand, Andre took a hold of her other. How could she let him go?

"I will get the word out that I am looking for photo opportunities in New York. Maybe all of U.S." He raised her hand and kissed her fingers. "I will be with you again, *chérie*."

"How likely is that Andre?" she asked, looking up into his beautiful chocolate eyes, also filled with sadness and longing.

He pursed his lips and blinked.

"We have to be positive, Lauren."

Her eyes grew more blurry as she approached the gate. They stopped. They delayed so much, everyone had already boarded.

"I have to go," she choked out.

She'd give anything not to have to say those words. She was hopelessly in love with her gorgeous Frenchman. The man who helped her overcome her fears at the Eiffel Tower. The man who lent his shoulder when she mourned the loss of her parents. The man who made love to her so sweetly she had no choice but to open her heart to love.

How was she going to go on when he lived thousands of miles away from her?

The ticket agent called for final boarding, and Lauren peeked a glance at her and saw her blatant stare.

A tear trickled down her cheek.

"I'll call you when I land," she whispered, and she hugged him close. Her throat felt tight, and her heart ached.

"*Oui*." Andre held her so tight he lifted her off the floor. "I love you, Lauren. Never forget that. Never forget me," he whispered to her.

She couldn't speak; she merely nodded and reached down for her carry-on. She proceeded toward the ticket agent and handed over her boarding pass. She looked back one last time to see the man she loved in anguish, watching her every move.

As she walked down the jet bridge, her legs felt terribly heavy. Her focus was dim because of the tears clouding her eyes. Her chest felt tight, and she struggled to get a complete breath.

Keep going. You must keep moving.

She could see the entrance to the plane what seemed like a mile ahead. She undoubtedly looked like a wreck, but she didn't have the heart to care.

A clamor of footsteps on the jet bridge shocked her, and her head shot upright. A gate agent proceeded up the jet bridge.

"Miss, we have to hurry to make our on-time departure," she said with a smile plastered on her face.

Lauren nodded because that was all she could muster to do, but the agent didn't look very pleased since her pace hadn't increased.

Well, my world is crumbling down around me, so you'll have to be patient.

She must have taken pity on Lauren because she gave a sad little smile. Lauren watched as the woman walked ahead.

As she approached the threshold of the plane, Lauren stepped on and stopped. The flight attendant looked at her expectantly, her eyebrows raised, and her hands clasped in front of her.

Lauren finished stepping onto the plane. The flight attendant cast a glance at her ticket.

"Fifth row here, Miss, on the right," she smiled as she pointed to the First Class seat.

Lauren licked her lips, held her bag on her shoulder, and sidled down the aisle. She avoided eye contact with any passenger. Anyone who wasn't otherwise occupied probably glared at her for keeping the plane at the gate.

Her breathing became labored as her lungs constricted. She held a hand over her heart; she felt it race.

She had the aisle seat, so she looped her bag off her shoulder and shoved it under the seat in front of her. Spots covered her vision, and she felt as if she might faint. She grabbed the seatbacks at each side of her and held her head down.

"Miss, are you alright?" the flight attendant asked, her face in a frown.

Lauren let go of the seatbacks and slid into her seat. She nodded and forced a smile as she reached for her seatbelt. She panted.

The flight attendant glanced back at the purser who was chatting with the gate agent.

After a moment, Lauren heard a thud and jumped. She knew what that meant—the airplane door had been closed.

The flight attendant hovered.

"Are you afraid of flying?"

"No. No."

Oh God. Please leave me alone. I just want to get home and cry for a decade.

"Charles," the agent called to the purser.

Charles walked over with his lips thinned to a line.

"What's up?"

"I think Miss Knight is having an anxiety attack," she spoke in a very low tone.

"I can't be here," Lauren breathed. Her lips moved on their own.

She looked again toward the front where the door was. What was she expecting to see? She wiped the tears that streamed down her cheeks.

Andre.

The purser asked her something about wanting a drink, but his voice sounded so distant as if she were in a tunnel.

Abruptly, the words from her aunt's letter screamed out in her head. *That's all I can ask of you and Colton. Have no regrets. Live life to the fullest.*

Lauren froze. The tears stopped. *Have no regrets.* But that's exactly what she was about to do, wasn't she? Create one big, nasty, heart-wrenching regret.

Why are you going back, Lauren? Really?

Her brother could survive on his own. He might need to downsize to a smaller apartment, but he could do that. And he still had his remodeling business. As for Regina, fuck her.

Geez! She had rarely said that word, but maybe it was long overdue. Surely she wouldn't miss a demeaning verbal thrashing the moment she landed in New York.

Really? What are you thinking? You have a man here whom you love and who loves you. And you've got an amazing opportunity to live and work in Paris.

The flight attendant looked down at Lauren; her thinly plucked eyebrows pinched together.

"Miss?"

"Um . . . I'm not going. Charles, I need to get off the plane. I need to get off the plane." The lightness in her words carried throughout her entire body.

The purser and the flight attendant looked at each other. Charles swiftly swiveled around and picked up the phone, probably to talk to the captain.

Lauren's heart raced. She unhooked her seatbelt and stood.

"Miss, please stay here a moment."

Lauren could faintly hear the purser's side of the conversation.

"No, I don't think she can make it . . . Yes . . . No . . . Yes, sir."

Please. Please let me go.

Charles hung up the phone and made direct eye contact with the flight attendant. Then he picked up the phone again. She strained to make out what he said. Something about "disarming the door".

Oh, God. Breath, Lauren.

She heard the door whoosh open. The flight attendant faced her again.

"You're free to go."

She scooped up her bag, edged past the agent and damn-near ran up the jet bridge. She shoved the heavy metal door. The gate area appeared clear. She searched for Andre. Her heart pounded in her chest. She whirled to the left.

She saw him ahead slowly walking down the wide of the airport toward the exit. His head down and his shoulders uncharacteristically slouched.

"Andre," she called. He didn't hear her. "Andre!"

CHAPTER EIGHTEEN

ANDRE STOPPED at hearing his name and spun around finding Lauren's eyes instantly through the crowd. He made his way toward her, his long legs eating up the distance between them.

She dropped her bag and jumped into his arms. She grabbed his face and her lips crushed his. He held her tight and latched onto her mouth in a desperate, passionate kiss.

She pulled herself impossibly closer, as if her life depended on it.

After several moments, she broke the kiss. She was long overdue in saying the words out loud.

"I can't go. I love you. I love you madly, and I don't want to be without you."

Initially his face showed disbelief, but her smile reassured him. The smile that crept over his lips was beautiful. His dimple, beautiful. How could she have thought of leaving all that?

"You're staying? Truly?"

She nodded feverishly. "Truly."

"*Chérie*, I love you." His hand grasped the nape of her neck and he brought his lips to hers for a kiss of eternity. Long, languid, sensual, and so full of love. After several minutes, he whispered over her lips, "Come home with me."

"*Oui*," she breathed back.

He carried her bag outside as they walked hand in hand. He opened the door to his car, and she climbed in. In an unexpected move, he pulled her face to his for another tongue kiss.

"I cannot have you away from me anymore," he said with a small, cautious smile on his face. He took a hold of her hand and held it the whole drive home.

Minutes later, they entered his apartment. She placed her bag on the floor in the middle of the room and rose to face him. He trained his eyes on her even as he locked the door and set his keys on the side table.

He strode to just in front of her and stopped, without touching any part of her.

"The thought of being without you nearly killed me."

A single finger rolled down her cheek to her neck and back up again. Her breath hitched at the sweet sensation.

"Tell me again, *chérie*."

"I'm staying."

His finger slid down her throat and slipped a button on her blouse.

"What will your brother think?" His finger lazed up and down her décolletage.

She thought for a second. "That I'm crazy. But I don't care." Her voice sounded breathy.

Another button unhooked.

"And what about your job?"

Think.

The anticipation was killing her. Her nipples peaked with every stroke of his finger.

"I don't want it. I . . . I can work here."

He slipped two buttons this time.

"And why are you staying?" His finger dipped into her cleavage.

She moaned.

"Because . . . I love you."

His lips curved. The look of utter satisfaction.

He slowly skimmed his fingers to her shoulders and pushed her blouse and her bra straps mid-way down her arm. Then he placed his fingers at the swell of her breasts and swirled over her skin and under the lace. He leaned down and, expecting a kiss, she gasped when his fingers pulled the satin down over her breasts, and his mouth sucked on one nipple. She cried out.

The moisture at her sex now soaked her panties. She wanted to touch him, rip off his shirt, feel his skin, but her arms were bound by her top and bra straps.

"Andre," she breathed as she let her head fall back.

He said nothing as he went down to his knees before her and reached to work her pants' button.

"Tell me again, *chérie*. How do you feel about me?"

His kisses began on her stomach and, after pulling on her pants, they continued down over her sex.

"I love you, Andre."

He pulled her pants to the floor and stroked her legs up and down. He slipped a finger under her panties at her bikini line.

"How do you know?" he asked.

"Andre," she begged.

"*Chérie*, do you know how I knew?" He wiggled a finger in, pulling on her stuck panties. He slid his finger softly over her wet lips.

"Ah." She felt light-headed with his ministrations.

"I knew because I couldn't think of anything—anything—when I was with you. And I couldn't think of anything but you when I wasn't with you. You make me smile and laugh. You find goodness in everything. You make me see a side of myself I didn't know existed." His finger slipped inside her core.

"Unh," she cried out. Her whole body trembled. She gripped his shoulders. A few rubs brought her orgasm to hover just under the surface.

He slid her panties down and held her pants so she could step out of them. He stood, and she watched as he yanked off his shirt and pushed off his jeans and briefs.

"Turn around, *chérie*."

She did, and he brought his naked body flush to the back of hers. He bound an arm around her waist. Then he bent his knees enough to stroke his cock over her weeping sex. Her hands felt for his rippled stomach—the first time she'd been able to touch his bare skin since they arrived.

"Chérie, you are clean and you just had your period. I have been tested, and I am clean. I'm taking you like this." His cock glided over her sex again.

Oh. "Yes, Andre." She trusted him; there was no question.

He continued to stroke her, wetting his cock with her essence. One hand covered her breast while his fingers toyed with the nipple.

"Ah," she sighed as her head fell back on his shoulder.

Sliding his hand from her waist, he parted her with two fingers and slowly, gingerly pushed into her wet swollen core. A glorious push of hot steel.

She tightened around him as her orgasm flew through her on his third thrust.

"Oh!"

He held her tight as she panted. He continued his glide, diving in and pulling back. Feeling his flesh pushing and pulling over hers brought another tightening of her pussy. He groaned in her ear, and he moved both hands to cup her achy, heavy breasts. Despite already having one orgasm, she felt another build deep inside her.

"Oh, God," she panted.

He increased his speed, and she hung on to his ass, digging her nails into his flesh as he thrust inside her deeper.

She felt his mouth at her neck.

"*Chérie, je viens*," he breathed over her skin and bit her gently as he pumped twice more before he began coming inside her.

The feeling of his cock twitching inside her tight channel brought her orgasm racing through her. He held tight so she wouldn't fall.

"Andre," she screamed out his name.

Boneless, they fell to the ground. Their breathing was the only sound heard.

Lauren lay on the floor with Andre's arms wrapped around her. She should be anxious and nervous, but all she could feel was relief. She knew she was right where she was supposed to be.

She pushed off the floor, pulling away from Andre, she straightened her shirt and returned to laying on his body—chest to chest.

His arms came around her.

"What are you thinking, *chérie*?"

"I'm thinking that I made the right decision. I don't have any of the details worked out, but it feels so right to be here with you."

He popped his head up to kiss her forehead. "We will work it out. And you are welcome to stay here with me as long as you want." His smile brought out the dimple in his cheek.

"You like that idea."

"I like very much the idea of you staying here with me. And I like the idea of coming home to you waiting for me. Or me waiting for you."

She bit down on her upper lip.

"Is it too soon? We haven't known each other very long."

"I know. Take as much time as you need. And if you would like to look for an apartment, I will help you. But someday, you will be here with me." He reached up to the sofa and pulled down the throw to cover them.

She nodded, then lay her head back on his chest. The emotion of the day left her drained, and she couldn't help closing her eyes. She felt incredibly comfortable lying on Andre's smooth chest; his heartbeat lulled her to sleep.

Lauren awoke a few hours later still lying on Andre's chest, with his muscular arms encased around her. She knew soon it would be time for her to get up and call her brother. She needed to tell him—she wasn't coming back to the states.

The apartment was almost dark now. She glanced at her watch. Andre stirred, so she lifted her head.

"Hi."

"Hi," he said giving her a sleepy smile.

"I'm going to call my brother now, okay?"

"*Oui.*"

She hopped up, grabbed her clothes and went to the bathroom. She borrowed his toothbrush since hers was still packed. In a suitcase, going to the US.

She returned to the great room and retrieved her phone out of her purse and powered it on. A voice message and a text appeared from Cole.

Call me when you get this, was all it read. And his voicemail said pretty much the same thing.

The phone rang. "Hello?"

"Cole, it's me. What's going on?"

"Lauren, . . . wait. Where are you?"

"I'm in Paris. What's going on?"

"I thought you were on your flight?" he understandably sounded confused.

"I'll tell you about it after your news. What's up?"

Andre came up behind her, brushed her hair off her neck and planted a kiss on her. Then another. He may not even realize how he sent tingles all over her body. *Would it always be like this?* She smiled.

"Lauren, you're not going to believe this. Regina called me this morning. I met her at the office. As you know, she sent a letter out to the entire clientele at L'Eclisse letting them know that I was not gay and that I'd been fired, therefore the situation was under control."

Lauren could hear a lightness to Cole's voice that wasn't there when last they spoke. She found herself tapping her foot, anxious to learn what Cole had to say.

"Right. She told me she was going to do that."

"Well, evidently *several* letters came in from clients stating they wished I hadn't been fired. That they appreciated my customer service and congeniality and didn't mind that I was straight. That I was a great replacement for you, and they hated to see me go."

"You're kidding," she exclaimed. She was sure Andre looked at her, seeing her bulging eyes, wondering what was going on.

"No. Regina read a few lines from the letters. Someone, I don't know who, mentioned I made her feel good while going through her divorce, which was appreciated. Someone else said they understood the reason for doing what we did, and they would be so lucky to have a brother willing to sacrifice for his family."

"Wow." Lauren's words sounded breathy, even to herself.

"Regina and I sat down and agreed I could stay on to fill in for you as long as necessary. So did you miss your flight? There's no rush to come back," he chuckled.

"Cole, I did miss my flight. Intentionally."

"What?"

"Cole, how did you like working at L'Eclisse?"

"Um, I liked it. Definitely more than I thought I would. Why? Lauren, what's going on?"

"Here's the thing." She sat down at Andre's kitchen table. "I don't want to come back to New York. I want to stay in Paris. I want to move to Paris."

"Oh, geez! Does this have anything to do with Andre?"

"Yes. It does." She looked up at the man who made her want to shout out to the world how wonderful love felt. He leaned against the kitchen countertop, tipped his head and watched her with his glowing, warm eyes.

"I've fallen in love. I didn't mean to, but I did. Aside from you—and you are *very* important to me—I have nothing really tying me to New York." The pitch of her voice changed. "I tried to get on the plane Cole, but I couldn't." She looked again at the man who'd turned her life upside down. She felt her eyes grow watery. "I suppose this doesn't make much sense. But I just hope you're not too mad at me."

Silence screamed across the line.

Cole finally spoke, "I'm not mad, Lauren. You *are* making sense. I met someone, so I get what you're going through."

She heard a softness in his voice.

"Really?" She was surprised only because of the coincidental timing. She knew it was just a matter of time for a woman to break through the walls he'd built up over the years and burrow into his heart. "Who is she?"

"She's Ace's little sister, Alexandra. Alex."

"Well, when I come back to New York to pack up my things, I'd love to meet her.

"You'll really like her. What about the apartment?"

"It's yours. Do as you wish. I'll have my name taken off the lease."

"Okay. Geez, sis. I can't believe this."

"I know. Sudden, huh? But it feels so right." She knew her brother would understand. "I'll call Regina tomorrow morning and tell her I'm not coming back. The job is yours if you want it."

"What are you going to do?"

"I'll find something here." She smiled feeling more resolute and comfortable with her decision now having spoken to Cole. "Go be with Alex. We'll talk later about the estate. I'll get your bank information and have the financial guys do the transfer when the house closes."

"Okay. Take care. I love you."

"I love you back. Bye." She disconnected the line, set the phone down and smoothed her lips between her teeth.

"How did it go?" Andre asked.

She focused on him and stood. She walked toward him as he opened his arms to her. She eagerly went and felt the warmth of his arms envelope her.

"It went well. He wasn't mad. He met someone and fell in love." She snorted. "I knew it was only a matter of time."

"For both of you, it seems."

She raised her head to meet his gaze. "Yes. Indeed."

"When will you go back to New York?"

"When you can come with me."

His lips curved. "I'd like that." He kissed her quickly but warmly. "How about I make us something to eat?"

She nodded.

Andre warmed quiche and bread, then sliced some fruit. They ate in amicable silence for a while, although she sensed something was on his mind.

After several minutes, Andre spoke. "It's been a few hours, Lauren. How do you feel?"

She furrowed her brows.

"How do you feel about staying here?" he asked in a low tone. He didn't know how to express that now he had fear. Fear that she could leave at any time, regretting her decision to stay permanently.

"I'm good." She shrugged a shoulder. "An outsider might think I was absolutely crazy, but I know I made the right decision." She reached across and laid her hand over his. "Why do you ask?"

He scratched the side of his jaw. "You have made a drastic decision. I," he glanced down briefly and took a breath, "I want to make sure you don't regret it."

She placed her napkin on the table and pivoted her chair to face him.

"Andre?"

"*Oui?*" He saw her eyes twinkle as she looked at him.

"You asked me why I love you." She took both his hands in hers. "It's simple. You make me want to learn and see more. You show me I can step outside my comfort zone and take a chance. You make me laugh." She smiled and smoothed her hand over his muscular chest. "And you make me feel so damn sexy," her voice dropped a hint.

She held his gaze intently. His tongue swiped his lower lip.

"You are damn sexy," he growled. Then in a swift move, he scooped her up and carried her to his bedroom. She shrieked. He laid her on the bed and whipped off his clothes and pulled her pants and panties off too. Would she always turn him on like this?

He lowered himself, covering his body with hers. He positioned his thigh between hers. His growing erection nudging her pussy.

He kissed her deeply as her hands wound around his neck.

"I am so very happy you decided to stay, *chérie*," he breathed over her lips.

"Me too, baby."

With his left hand, he caressed her right thigh and bent her knee, bringing it to the side of his torso. Then reaching beneath, he brushed a finger over her sex, still wet from his semen.

She arched her back, and her eyes fluttered shut. He tilted his pelvis and brought the head of his cock to her entrance and slowly pushed in. She gripped his shoulders and bowed her neck.

"Ah," she moaned.

As he moved slow and deliberately, he asked her, "Tell me again, *chérie*."

"I love you," she pumped her hips in time with his.

"Again."

"I love you, Andre," she said louder. "Ah."

He drove into her fully. He sped his pace and felt his face getting hot.

"I can't live without . . . you," she panted.

He crashed his lips down over hers and kissed her deeply, tongues tangling.

"Surrender, *cherie*."

With his words, her orgasm hurtled through her, and she cried out. She was positively beautiful when she came.

His balls drew up, and a spectacular energy rocketed throughout his body. He groaned and collapsed over her, keeping the weight on his forearms.

"I love you, *cherie*. I cannot live without *you*," he whispered into her neck.

CHAPTER NINETEEN

LAUREN PUT THE finishing touches on her makeup when her cell phone rang. It was Corinne.

"Hello, Corinne."

"Hi, Lauren. Do you have a few minutes? I've received two offers on your house, and I'd like to discuss them with you."

"Well, Corinne, I'm still in Paris. How about we meet?"

"Oh, that would be wonderful. When is a good time?"

They arranged a time later that afternoon to meet to Corinne's office.

Lauren wondered when she would get the call from Corinne telling her she had an offer. Now, she had two. What a surprise. And truly, Lauren should be jumping for joy.

Instead, she had other ideas.

She walked into the living room where Andre was focused on something on his computer. She waited for him to look up.

"Hey, *chérie*. Sit." He patted the sofa next to him. "What would you like to do today?"

She licked her lips. "Andre, I have a few things to take care of. I need to meet with Mr. Bernard and Corinne. Can we reconnect for dinner tonight? I can be back here around five."

"*Oui*. Of course. I have a conference call this afternoon and some work to do, so five will be perfect." He smiled.

She smiled and leaned in to kiss him. She loved how easygoing he was. He was the type of man who could take life as it came, one step at a time. The type of man who would make a good husband and father.

Andre watched Lauren grab her purse and head out his apartment door. Now that she was gone, he had phone calls to make—his parents and his sister.

His mother answered the phone on the second ring. They chatted in French for a while, and she told him she missed him.

"Mother, I'm going to come and visit you very soon."

"Ah, yes. That would be wonderful, Andre," she burst out. "Your father would love it, too."

"And I will be bringing a friend."

"A friend? A girlfriend?"

"Yes. Her name is Lauren. She's American. I met her four weeks ago. She's amazing, Mom. You will love her."

"Oh, Andre. I'm so happy for you. And if you love her, I know I will love her."

He smiled. He hadn't even told her his feelings for Lauren, but how well mothers knew their sons.

"When are you coming?"

He told her about Lauren's reason to be in Paris and her plan to stay. They would need to plan around her schedule and his work in Pamplona.

After he spoke with Lauren, they could determine the best day to get away so he could introduce her to his parents. He knew without a doubt that they would get along well. One day they would be her in-laws, and she should meet them, the sooner, the better.

Lauren's mind raced. The last twenty-four hours had been a blur. She hadn't even thought about the house. Why would she sell that beautiful house when she was moving to Paris? She needed a place to live anyway. God, did she really need a house that size? She would if she planned to have children.

The thought made her smile. She could envision children running around in the backyard, playing on the swings, begging Daddy to throw them in the air. Andre. A shiver rushed through her body. She could imagine that—children with Andre. He would make an amazing father. She knew that to her core. Her eyes grew misty.

Would he like that? She had to believe he would.

First things first. She needed to talk to Corinne.

She paid the cabbie and rushed to Corinne's office.

"Lauren. So good to see you. Please come in. Have a seat. I was surprised when you said you were still here."

"Yes, well, Corinne, there's a reason for that. Things have changed." She took a deep breath.

"Shortly after arriving in Paris, I met someone, and as foolish as it may sound, I've fallen in love."

Corinne smiled and tilted her head as she listened.

"In fact, I decided not to return home. I'm going to live here. I'm going to stay in Paris."

She waited for Corinne to look shocked or upset or even quizzical, but it never came.

"Lauren, I'm very happy for you."

"Well, you may not be so happy when I tell you I don't want to sell the house."

"No, I'm still happy." She leaned forward and cupped the back of Lauren's hand. "That house needs you. It needs to be filled with love. And you are just the person to do it."

Oh my God! Her mouth gaped. "I thought for certain you would be upset."

"Not at all. I'm very happy for you and your new love. I will simply get back to the two prospective buyers and let them know the home is no longer on the market."

Lauren's heart rate jumped. She was one step closer to having her dream come true.

She stood. "Thank you, Corinne," and she dashed out the door.

The taxi dropped Lauren a block from Mr. Bernard's office at a city park. She found a place to settle and dialed her brother's number.

"Hello?"

"Hi, Cole. Do you have a minute?"

"Hey, Lauren. Sure, I'm just getting ready for work. What's going on?"

She took a deep breath. "Cole, I was planning to find an apartment in Paris to live, at least for the time being. But . . . how would you feel about me living in Aunt Rosie's house?"

"Wow. I think that's a great idea. It makes sense. I mean it's been paid for. Free housing." She could hear his smile.

"Not exactly free, Cole. You own half of it." She let it sink in the gravity of what she was saying.

"So?"

She wrinkled her brows. "So, I need to buy you out of your half if it's going to be my new home."

"Okay. We'll figure out the financial stuff later. Look, Lauren, some of the assets from the estate are already appearing in my brokerage account. I'm tickled pink to not have to worry about money again, even without the proceeds from the house." He inhaled. "I am grateful for what you've done to make this happen for us. Don't worry about me. Get settled, and we can work out the details later."

His gesture humbled her. "Thanks, Cole. That means a lot to me."

"What does Andre think?"

She smiled. "He doesn't know yet. I'm going to tell him tonight." She had been scheming.

"You sound happy, sis," he said in a low tone.

"Thanks. I am. Well, I'm going to talk to the attorney and then make my way to Andre's."

"Okay. Love you."

"Love you back," she disconnected the line.

"Lauren! What an unexpected surprise. I thought you'd be back in the States by now," Mr. Bernard called out.

She took the seat in his office that he offered her.

"Yes, well, Mr. Bernard, things have changed on my end. I won't going back. At least not permanently. I plan to stay in Paris. In my aunt's house."

The smile that came across his face was brilliant and wide.

"Lauren, that is excellent news. I'm sure you will be happy."

"There's more."

He nodded.

"I would like to buy a spa. I managed a spa in New York for years and thoroughly enjoyed it. Someday I will buy a spa in Paris, and I would like you to help me with that."

His brows rose. "Yes, of course."

"Also, since I will be living here, I need get a visa and work on my citizenship. Hopefully dual citizenship, if that's possible."

He nodded, but stayed silent.

She smoothed her lips together and took in a breath.

"I'll call my financial advisors tomorrow regarding keeping the funds local, instead of transferring them to the States."

His silence was starting to make her nervous.

"Mr. Bernard, is there something wrong?"

He blinked a few times and leaned toward her a few inches.

"No, *mademoiselle*. Nothing is wrong." His eyes softened. "I am so proud of you, and I have no doubt your parents and your aunt would be as well."

He smiled and shook his head. "I would love nothing more than to help you get settled here in Paris.

You deserve every happiness, and I think you will be happy here."

My goodness! She was touched again by generous words. She felt like she was in the presence of . . . an uncle, not an attorney she met just four weeks ago.

"Thank you, *Monsieur* Bernard. I'll keep you posted as things transpire."

The excitement in her plan kicked in once again. She felt the adrenaline pump through her veins. She rose and clasped his hand.

"Okay, Lauren. I'll speak with you soon."

"Goodbye," she spun around to head to the door. And to Andre.

CHAPTER TWENTY

LAUREN WALKED into the apartment with a look on her face that read relaxed and happy. She must have had a good day. There was an incredible feeling of peace that flowed through Andre seeing his love walk through his front door. He rose from the kitchen table and crossed to her.

"Hi," she greeted him.

He took her face in his hands and brought his lips down to hers for a slow, sensual kiss. "Hi."

"Wow. I could get used to that." She smiled.

"Good. I want you to. How did your day go?"

"Good. I have an idea. Let's go out for dinner." He noticed the twinkle in her eyes.

"That sounds great."

"Okay, let me get cleaned up and we'll leave."

"This early?"

"Yes." She smiled a devious little smile and pivoted away toward the bedroom. His *chérie* had something up her sleeve. The corner of his lips curved.

They walked to the car, and as he reached for the door, she placed her hand over his. "May I drive?"

His lips quirked. "You want to drive the Matchbox?"

She smiled fully. "Yes, please."

He nodded. "All right," he held up the keys and dropped them in her palm.

She swung around to the driver's side and sat. Without putting the key in the ignition, she swiveled to face him.

"Just one little thing to start our evening, Andre," she slipped off a scarf from around her neck. "You have to cover your eyes with this."

He unsuccessfully held back a grin. "Really?"

"It's the rule if you want to go out with me tonight."

He ran a tongue over his teeth. "All right."

He took the blue scarf, covered his eyes and tied it in the back.

"No peeking," she said.

He smiled. "Okay."

They took off and, truth be told, he was excited about what she planned to show him. He couldn't tell where they were going, or even in which direction. He definitely got the impression that they were leaving the city because he no longer felt the car turning corners. After about twenty-five minutes, they stopped.

"Stay there. I'll come get you," she commanded.

He heard her door open, then felt his open and her hand reach in for his arm.

"Watch your step."

"Ha. Ha." He felt the curb with his foot, stepped fully onto it and rose from the car. He had to chuckle. How long was she going to keep him blindfolded? She guided him a few steps and shut the car door.

She brought herself in front of him, her hands clutching his upper arms. She leaned up to place a sweet kiss on his lips. Her breathing seemed accelerated, like she was excited or nervous.

"I love you, Andre," she whispered over his lips.

His heart expanded. He knew she did, but it felt good every time he heard it from her.

"I made a decision." She turned him and slipped off his blindfold.

He squinted and blinked in the bright sunlight. As his eyes adjusted, he saw they were in front of her aunt's house. It took him a minute to digest her words, but he got it.

"You're keeping the house," he said looking down at her.

She nodded. "I know it's a big house, but I love it. I can't bring myself to sell it knowing I'll be moving to Paris. Let's go inside." She took his hand, unlocked the door, and entered the foyer.

"*Chérie*, I'm so happy for you," he said as he wrapped his arms around her and pulled her in close. "This is a wonderful house."

She smoothed her lips in between her teeth. "Andre—"

"*Chérie*," he addressed her fears about not including him, "I will keep my place. I make no presumptions."

She noticeably relaxed in his arms. "Thank you for understanding. I have been through so much this month. I don't want to rush anything."

She adored him and wouldn't make him wait too long. But he knew what she had gone through lately. It was an emotional and growth-filled time. Her decisions about the future wouldn't be rushed. For she knew, after Andre moved in, he would want to marry her. And God help her, she wanted that too.

"Of course."

"There is something else. Come. Let's sit."

He followed her into the living room and sat with her on the sofa.

"I didn't tell you but my aunt's inheritance is quite substantial. I have the house and will need to buy out Cole, but otherwise we have just under three million dollars to split between the two of us."

His eyes widened. "*Incroyable*," he breathed.

"I would like to take some of that money and buy a spa in Paris someday. Not now, but someday. If I'm my own boss, I will have freedom," she held his hands in hers, "freedom to travel with my boyfriend." A shy smile graced her face.

"*Chérie*." He leaned forward and gave her a soft, swift peck on the lips. "That would be wonderful."

She smoothed her hair behind an ear. "Are you okay with . . . all of this?"

"*Oui*. Why wouldn't I be? As long as you are here with me," he kissed the backs of her hands, "I don't care what you do and where you live." His voice dropped lower and softer. "From the moment I laid eyes on your graceful face, I knew I had to be with you."

Her eyes became clouded. "Andre, you are everything I want in a man." She leaned in to hold on to his face and kiss him deeply.

He moaned, and shifted them to lie flat on the sofa, with her underneath him. "My only question is why is it taking us so long to christen this house?"

She giggled and squirmed, feigning to push him off her. "No, Andre."

But with his next sensual kiss—the kiss that did her in from day one—she knew she didn't have the strength to fight him. And why not christen what would one day be their house?

EPILOGUE

Three Weeks Later

"I love waking up next you," Lauren whispered as Andre kissed her neck and shoulders while he stroked her torso.

"I love *you*," Andre replied and rolled her onto her back.

Lauren and Andre had arrived in New York the day before and enjoyed a relaxing morning lounging in bed. Andre had slipped out of bed to make coffee, and because he couldn't seem to keep his hands off her body, the coffee now sat getting cold.

"Andre," she breathed.

He kissed his way down to her stomach and slipped a finger to her core. His touch set her skin on fire. She ran her fingers through his hair and down his back.

He lifted his head and hovered over her to press his lips to hers. Her moan escaped into his mouth when he slid two fingers into her.

"*Chérie*, you feel incredible."

"Mmm," she moaned again.

The climax that flew through her was fast and unexpected. Andre knew just how to touch her.

"God, Andre," she breathed.

He slipped out and rolled them onto their sides.

"Andre, now that I'm living in Paris, you are going to have to help me with my French, *monsieur*," she said playfully.

"Ah, *oui*." He nodded. "First try: Andre, *je t'aime*."

She smiled. "Andre, *je t'aime*."

"Next, *je veux être avec toi pour toujours*."

She tipped her head. "I don't think this is helping."

"And lastly, *fais moi l'amour*," he said in a low tone as his eyes heated.

She licked her lips, pushed him over onto his back, and straddled him.

"Andre, *fais moi l'amour, s'il te plait*," she breathed as she moved herself over his cock.

He groaned and grabbed her face bringing her to his lips for a deep kiss.

She reached between them, held his cock in her hand and shifted her weight to slide him inside her. She sighed.

"*Chérie*, you make me happy." His voice was soft and sincere as he stroked his hands over her body. "I want to try something. Turn around and lie back on me."

Her eyes sparkled at him. "Okay." She carefully pivoted, facing the opposite direction, and laid back on him, her head to the side of his.

"Now, arms overhead," he whispered in her ear.

She did as he commanded and felt his hands caress breasts and tease her nipples. A zing of sensation rippled through her sex. He slid his hands down and spread her legs open. With a single finger, he glossed over her clit while continuing to move inside her.

She moaned aloud and braced her hands against the headboard.

They moved together as one. Their bodies always seemed in sync.

She let her eyes fall closed as Andre applied more pressure. She could feel she was close.

"God, Andre . . . don't stop."

Their breathing intensified. After another moment, she came and cried out. He followed shortly after.

She rested on his torso while he wrapped his arms around her tightly.

"Beautiful," he murmured into her hair.

They dozed for several minutes before Lauren stirred and took the quiet moment to watch Andre sleep. He looked beautiful and peaceful. His muscular chest rose and fell lightly with his breath. His dark eyelashes fanned over his eyes. She could watch him all day. My, she thought, how life can change on a dime.

He awoke slowly, and instantly smiled at her watching him.

"What are you doing?"

"Watching the most handsome man I know."

He rolled to his side and faced her. She leaned forward and kissed his beautiful lips.

"What would you like to do today?" he asked.

"Let's go to the spa. I'd like to see the progress. Then I should do a bit of packing."

"Whatever you want."

It was nearly lunchtime when Andre and Lauren arrived at L'Eclisse. Cole greeted them right away.

"Hey, sis. Hey, Andre." He kissed her cheek and leaned in to shake Andre's hand. "You guys sleep okay? How's the jet lag?"

"I'm feeling great, Cole," she said as her sight traveled the lobby of the spa. "And this place looks awesome."

"Yeah, it's coming together well. You can see we moved the reception desk." He motioned with an arm. "This wall will partition the open area." He walked past the newly created wall further into the spa. "And here we will add a door of frosted glass and another wall to create a hallway leading back to the office."

"This looks great," Andre chimed in.

"Regina has a decorator coming Monday to review wall colors and the like."

"How's she doing?" Lauren asked.

Cole grinned. "She's good. We have an understanding now." He nodded.

Lauren smiled. "Good. Well, can you break for lunch?"

"No, I really can't, but how about we meet for dinner tonight? The four of us."

"Sounds good to me. Where is Alex?"

"She has play rehearsal, but she'll be free tonight."

"Great. I'll make reservations. By the way, thanks again for staying with Alex. You didn't have to do that."

"Are you kidding?" Cole exclaimed. "Alex loves that I'm staying at her place for once." He grinned.

Cole said goodbye to his sister and Andre. Andre seemed like a first-rate guy. The kind of guy Cole hoped Lauren would end up with some day.

Cole finished up at the spa at five and made his way to Alex's apartment.

The landlady, Marguerite, had her door open, so he called out. "Hello, Marguerite."

"Hi, Cole. Your sister made it back?"

"Yes, ma'am. Of course, she's only here for a week before returning to France with her man."

She sighed. "How exciting," she beamed.

He paused a few steps up. "Marguerite, you need to have Hank take you to Paris."

"Ya' think?" she cooed.

"Definitely. Life's too short. Ya' got savor it while you can." He paused before he turned to climb the stairs. "I better get cleaned up before Alex comes home. Good night."

"'Night," she called after him.

He went to the closet to pull out a clean pair of slacks and a shirt, and laid them on the bed. With several minutes to spare, he collapsed in the family room chair to chug a beer. His mind rolled back to the last few weeks, and all that had transpired with Alex. He could still chuckle aloud at how she honed in on the fact that he was straight.

That followed by the whole fiasco with Eric. Cole was so proud of her for standing up to him. Hopefully, the dirt bag learned his lesson and wouldn't torment any women again. Cole shook his head and sighed.

He heard the door click and turned to see Alex walking through the apartment door. She smiled at him.

"Hi," she said.

He rose and crossed to her. He set her purse on the table, then cupped her face and lowered his lips to hers. Her tongue moved against his like they were made for each other.

He broke the kiss, slid his hands to her waist and tugged on her shirt. "How was rehearsal?"

"Good." She tracked his every move.

"We have seven-thirty reservations at DeShay's with Lauren and Andre. I was about to take a shower." He pulled her closer by her jeans' waistband and went to work on her button and zipper.

"Okay," she replied warily.

"So," he continued as he bent and whipped off her jeans and her shoes, "hair wet or dry?"

She stood frozen with her mouth agape. He grabbed her shirt hem and brought it over her head.

"Alexandra?"

"Um . . . dry. Dry hair."

"Then you better get a clip or something."

Her eyes went wide, and she scurried into the bedroom wearing only her bra and panties. He shed his clothes and followed her. Right as she got her hair off her back, he scooped her up over his shoulder.

She shrieked. "Cole! Put me down!"

"No way, sunshine. I have you to myself for an hour," he declared.

"You just 'had me' this morning, love. Now put me down."

"Okay." He did as she commanded and set her down in the shower, underwear be damned.

"Ah!" she screeched when the cold water hit her luscious body. "It's freezing!"

He stepped in behind her and murmured in her ear, "I'll make it a priority to get you warm then."

He removed her bra, letting it fall to the shower floor, and rained kisses over her neck and shoulders. His hands glided up her torso to cup her breasts. She sighed and let her head fall back on his shoulder.

He nudged his erection between her legs.

"Cole, you are so wonderful to come home to." Her hands reached behind and cupped his ass cheeks.

"Yeah?"

He moved his right hand to play with her sex, eliciting a squeeze of his ass. He moved a finger through her wet sex.

"Perhaps, then, you should move in with me."

"Mmm," was her noncommittal answer. He would try harder then.

He slipped her panties off and lifted her leg to place her foot on the edge of the tub. He leaned down more to stroke her core, spreading her slick moisture anywhere he knew would light her nerves.

She moaned.

"You could move in with me, help me redecorate after Lauren takes her stuff. We can cook together, watch stupid movies together, and stay up until all hours talking, getting to know each other."

"Talking?" Her words were breathy.

"Yes. Of course. Like we are now. And sometimes my fingers might be inside you," he said as he drove two fingers into her tight channel.

She audibly moaned.

"Other times it will be my very eager cock."

He could feel her muscles tremble. She was close.

"I could wake you in the morning, in the same way." He gently pulsed and twisted his fingers. "How does that sound?"

She whimpered.

He continued his pleasurable ministrations, and Alex began to tremble.

"You have my heart, Alex. Now I want yours," he whispered in her ear.

Before she could respond, he pushed his fingers in farther and smoothed his thumb over her throbbing clit. She gripped the shower curtain, her body tensed before she cried out as the orgasm raced through her.

He pulled his fingers away and spun her around to kiss her feverishly, deeply. He then lifted her and dove into her because he couldn't wait another second.

"Cole." Her eyes closed.

"Say yes, Alex. I don't want anyone else. Only you."

"Ah," she moaned as he continued his pace with her. She opened her eyes. "Yes, Cole. Yes. I'll move in with you."

He smiled. They both released together, and the calmness settled them. They kissed and held each other for long moments.

***

The hostess led the group to a quiet, candle-lit table in one of Soho's finer restaurant. A pianist played soft, elegant music. Andre laced his fingers through Lauren's and held her hand on his lap under the table cloth.

After water and bread had been delivered, the waitress arrived to take drink orders.

"I think tonight is a celebration of sorts," Cole spoke first. "And although I'm a beer drinker, I'd like to order a bottle of champagne to toast. Are you guys fine with that?"

Alex gave him a knowing smile. "That sounds great," she said.

"Sure," Lauren agreed.

The group chatted over appetizers and throughout dinner.

"So let me get this straight. This Eric character quit the next day?" Lauren asked with surprise in her voice and her eyes narrowed.

"Yes. That Monday," Alex replied.

"Unbelievable."

"Eric must have been embarrassed because I was just about to tell my boss all about the dirtbag, when he quit."

Alex shook her head and pursed her lips.

Cole reached over and, taking a hold of her hand, brought it to his lips and kissed it sweetly.

"I hope I never see that guy's face again," Cole murmured.

Dinner lasted hours. The group finished the champagne and a bottle of wine, then ordered two desserts to share with decaf coffee. They chatted about the spa, Alex's play, Andre's job, Paris, Cole and Lauren's aunt's house, which is now Lauren's. Finally, as the last of the other diners left, the four decided to call it a night. Lauren scampered over to Cole and took a hold of his arm.

"Meet me for breakfast tomorrow? How about Ground Support at nine o'clock?" she asked.

"Sure," he replied. "I'll see you there."

Everyone said their goodnights and parted.

"What was that about?" Andre asked her.

"I wanted to meet with Cole, just the two of us, and go over a few things tomorrow morning. We're meeting for breakfast. Is that okay?"

"*Oui*, of course. We should have them over for dinner sometime? I'd love to cook."

"Andre, that would be wonderful. And I promised to take you sightseeing."

He leaned down and kissed the tip of her nose. "Not to worry, *chérie*. We have time for that," he gave his dazzling smile.

His smile made her insides shimmer. She smiled back at him.

The next morning, Cole sat at the coffeehouse and waited for Lauren. He knew they had much to talk about.

She strolled in carrying books, photo books.

"Hey," she said

"Hey. How are you? I got you a latte and a blueberry muffin."

"Thanks. I'm real good. How about you?"

He had the feeling there was more expected with the answer to that question than fine.

"I'm doing well. Better now that things are settled with Regina."

She nodded. "I'm sorry I put you through that."

He held up a finger. "No need to apologize. Everything happened for a reason, did it not?" He let out a breath. "If you hadn't left me in charge of the spa, I may not have met Alex."

She tipped her head in confusion.

"I didn't have cufflinks to wear to work, so I called Aidan to borrow some. Alex was staying with him at the time."

"Oh, crap," she smiled. "I knew I forgot something."

He smiled and nodded.

"She's terrific, Cole. I'm so happy for you. For both of you."

"Thanks, Lauren. She's the real deal. And she's all I want in a woman." He was inclined to say something else, but decided to keep those thoughts to himself for a while.

"And Andre seems like a good guy."

She smiled. "He is. He's everything I could hope for—kind, patient, loving. He's definitely The One."

She inhaled.

"Look, I found these photo books at Aunt Rosie's house." She turned one around to face him. "I thought you might like to look at them."

As he flipped through the pages, she continued, "I don't know where the photo books are that we had at the house, but I suspect Uncle Gary and Aunt Doris took them as a way of protecting us."

"Hmm," he murmured as he flipped through the pages of wonderful photos of his parents, and he and his sister growing up. They brought back a lot of memories.

"You can take them with you. When you come to Paris to visit, there are more I can show you," she said with a small smile.

"Thanks, Lauren. I'd like to look at these." He closed the book and stacked them off to the side.

She sipped her coffee, and then nodded. "There's the matter of the house, Cole."

"I know." He looked up from his plate. "I've given it some thought. Have the attorney draw up a document listing the fair market value of the house and the buyout price for my half. We will both sign it, and you pay me back when you can, as you can."

Her eyebrows came together, and she tipped her head.

Cole leaned forward in his chair.

"Lauren, everything has been transferred into my account now. It is something I never expected to see, at least before I turned sixty. This was unreal, and . . . unexpected. I don't need the money from the house." He shrugged his shoulder.

"Eventually it will be good when I have kids to send to college." He smiled, then reached a hand and cupped hers. "I have no doubt, you'll pay me my part. I don't want you to feel beholden to a payment schedule. There's no need to be stressed if you were late, or whatever. It's just not worth it. If there is anyone on the planet that I know will pay me back, it's you."

Her eyes grew misty. "I will."

"I know it." He leaned back in her chair. "Focus on getting settled, and looking into a spa you'd like to buy."

She nodded.

"Alex and I are already thinking about trying to come out to visit during Christmas and New Year's. Would that work for you two?"

"Yes. That would be perfect."

They chatted about the house and how easily it could accommodate guests. Her face lit up when she talked about the house. Cole knew she had made the right decision by keeping it.

They nearly finished breakfast when Lauren spoke, "There's one last thing."

"Okay."

She licked her lips. "We need to make a pact."

"A pact?"

"Yes. Aunt Rosie said in her letter her biggest regret was not seeing Mom enough before she died. She let the distance come between them. We need to make sure that doesn't happen to us."

He felt his body relax. He was so glad to hear her words. He and his sister were tight. Nothing would break his heart faster than knowing they had drifted apart.

He stuck out his hand. "Deal. Let's shake on it."

She smiled and stuck out her hand.

"Besides," he continued. "I'm willing to bet that you guys will have kids before we do, and I'm really gonna want to spoil my nieces and nephews while I can," he said with a grin on his face.

She threw back her head and chuckled. "Don't count on it, little brother."

They cleared the table and made their way to the front door. "By the way, we're gonna have you and Alex over for dinner. Andre wants to cook."

"That sounds awesome. We'll be there."

"Great," she wrapped her arms around him. "Love you."

"Love you back."

Thank you for reading.

Please consider leaving a review.

Mia London Books:

Perfect Seduction

Perfect Surrender

Life to the Max

ABOUT THE AUTHOR

Mia London loves to write.
After reading fiction for years, she decided it was finally time to put those images and scenes floating around in her head down on paper.

She is a huge fan of romance, highly optimistic, and wildly faithful to the HEA (happily ever after). Her goal is to create a fantasy you will enjoy with characters you could love.

She lives in Texas with her attentive, loving, super-model husband, and perfectly behaved, brilliant children. Her produce never wilts, there are no weeds in her flowerbeds and chocolate is her favorite food group.

www.Facebook.com/MiaLondonAuthor
www.MiaLondon.com
Email: mia@mialondon.com

9 780990 527459